OFF THE

DRIBBLE

A NOVEL BY

THE GOVENOR

OFF THE DRIBBLE

Copyright© 2022 Joseph Flowers
ISBN: 979-8-9856184-3-3 (Paperback)
ISBN: 979-8-9856184-4-0 (eBook)

Books in quantities may be purchased for sell by contacting publishers:
www.houserepspublishing.com
1401 21st. St.
Site.6325
Sacramento Ca, 95812

Facebook: Joseph Gov Flowers
Instagram: @thegove.s.o

Published and printed in the United States Of America.

Thanks much Reader,

Hope you enjoyed the book to the fullest as I am humbly appreciative you have shared these thoughts with me. You happen have few extra seconds after you've finished reading it, please upon if you do not mind leave uh' quick review. Whether you're uncertain or pressed for time, that's fine; you may still leave the quick rankings utilizing the stars, I'm always interested to learn my viewers thoughts and how improving my craft.

www.houserepspublishing.com

Acknowledgments

The highest praises and glory upon mighty heavenly father above sending his blessings, insights and thoughts as a Gods gift upon planet Earth. "John 3:16 versus" Thanks much to my grandparents, Moms and Pops, Uncle's and Aunties, my multitude of brothers, Sisters, Nieces, and Nephews. Unk loves you much. I dedicate this to anyone that has help raise and guided upon my pathways. And those whom contributed in person and the non physical forms throughout my life. Never forgotten, you my best friend out there Beyond.

GROWING UP IN EAST
OAKLAND, IS A STORY
IN ITSELF

OFF THE DRIBBLE

A Novel By

THE GOVENOR

Chapter 1

MONEY IS NOT AS DIFFICULT TO GET AS IT'S HARDER HOLDING ONTO

Growing up in Oakland, California, is a story in itself. Not to discredit being baptized to the game the day I gleamed at a shotgun appearing outta the trunk of a 1970'ish Cadi Seville. At four years of age, still although too young to fight back, I could only ask the questions, "How would God let something as gruesome and cruel happen near the sight of an innocent child's presence?" Only thing heard was one shot outta the twelve gauge pump, and blood flew everywhere. Soon, my Auntie "Kennedy" gets abandoned, placed into a plastic bag, and thrown inside a garbage bin to die. Her ex-boyfriend, Zeus, then sped off, likely thinking she'd not survive the tragic incident. Luckily, having splendid instincts, I counteracted and readily dove right in without even thinking further, ripping the bag open. I gladly found Auntie Kennedy kicking, alive and breathing, screaming for help. We were approximately two blocks from Grandma's house in the deep trenches of East Oakland, 10th Avenue, and I hauled Azz quickly as these two wheels would lift. As I approached the front door of Grandma's house, was outta of breath, dripping in tears, running fast enough to read the time.

I yelled, "Grandma, Grandma! They just shot Auntie Kennedy." Before this incident, she and Zeus had been dating for several years, now what excited her about him thus, honestly, I wouldn't know had it stared right into my eyes. But thankfully, applying such youthful wisdom, which was gathered from being up underneath my older siblings and Moms, I managed. Even at my young tender age, surprisingly, I knew how to react in a shocking life-death situation to have alerted Grannie's assistance to the area in a timely fashion. My auntie Kennedy lay there helplessly, eyes opened with blood pouring everywhere. Upon getting to the scene, she hadn't quite grasped that Grannie and I were there at her assistance to save the day. She was furiously quite surprised.

Auntie painfully grunted aloud, "Nephew, get Auntie some help." She helplessly repeated this over maybe thirty times, loudly but slurredly. When she opened her eyes and noticed us, that's when she yelled and cried out to Grannie, who was alarmed, but I couldn't blame that on her, looking on as Auntie's pain appeared unbreathable.

"Momma, please! Zeus knows who shot me." As I continued listening while she pled for her life, to this day, I'm fighting with my internal throngs of her pains and cries on replay over and over in my mental treasury, as if it happened just yesterday. Thank God for us making our way to Highland General Hospital timely enough for her to have had a healthy surgery.

Years later, Zeus was reportedly found to have been non- responsible; who had done it, I wouldn't know. But it's believed Zeus was a debadgitized New Jersey State Trooper, which, as I gauge for the unanswered questions for closures, I'm partly forgiven as the Bible teaches us. But, the other level of the game almost more often peeks it's outta that Ozone layer, but the side the streets raise, born go-getters– where revenge warrants anytime a particular line crossed between obligations and morals upon principles. Although I haven't digested the full effects of his actions yet, since that day kinda something forewarns that he's hawked my every step. And I do wonder whether or not observations of my life through the none other untainted visuals were warranted, irrespective of close and personal or afar distance. Kinda in my opinion provides an opportunity to facet this hustling mentality he's helped rebound from a horrific eye-opening of events cause, Lord who knows!

Overcoming her tragedy had everlasting effects as my world of torments. I haven't had the same topography for the betterment or negates, yet the quest I'm living for begs for the least faintest clarified signs. "Why Auntie?" But only in good measures, I've asked. Mindful, I'm working on teaching myself how to leave yesterday's pains as peaceful severances, but I'm not the easiest or greatest at saying goodbyes. You'd be throttled. I understood at such a tendered age how money meant power and respect. Who wouldn't have had voiced, for it's only our human nature's formalities.

Now mind you, if I've opted no reprises of waivers, just so you know, my hustles are forever the epical upon my growth and cultural shock barriers. In so many ways, I am nonrestrictive. I practice the utmost desires, living wholesomely and mindful the things that I'm unable to change. Having been born under the name of "Maxwell Aswad Pixar", upon I grew up in East Oakland, referred to as da' trenches the deep. Whereas it's often move first, ask questions last. It's my inference Zeus deserves to taste samples of this hustler, which attributes his growth creations to the same reasons the hood retorts the art of actions.

Having dangled like any other young youth growing up in poverty, dabbled in most hustles even above the street levels, which includes helping older folks at grocery stores and assisting their bags inside their vessels. At times, if getting lucky, I'd earn fifty cents for the helping hands and a habit that I loved to endeavor, breeding pets. Often though, I wasn't able to afford those hobbies, but you know I hustled my heart out getting that dough right.

Grannie hated my projects but I fought the reasoning with G'moms. The hardest was convincing her to not shelf those youthful desires of mine. At the same time, she urged me to engage with other more rewarding life-skill ventures like attending school, doing of daily activities, reading books, not forgetting housework chores. Still, nothing mattered more besides the things I enjoyed investing my time doing. But I wouldn't listen had my life depended on it. Living that adrenaline even after not having such good ol' days on the hustle, my mother Margaret understood and hadn't minded pitching her baby a coin or ah' few bucks to keep my hobbies afloat. Maybe that's the reason our bounds were reflective, not the slightest bits ignoring the fact she thankfully nurtured giving me life. But look how I fended her baby sister's life, which only induced our bond. Boy, that was too much for TV. Nonetheless, it was bar-by-bar on another plateau; a fragile subject, but it's lively with dispositions of our family's unspeakable love.

Absent a father most days, yet Momma handled both obligations well. We weren't pressed needing much and held tight like ricochet and bulletproof. The values are unmeasurable. Whenever she veered upon travel, you found her baby right sideline kicked near! Regularities panned out with uh' few untasteful setbacks of growing up without Pops not around much, kinda' in the fields. Yet Momma rebounded, building our family's foundation. It was during these years Pops extended his dutiful services to the Navy. Inarguably, those were ultimately my neediest youthful years. Non-reversible and important phases going through life, despite that we were air tight. Most of the times, momma's levels upon provenience were amazing. She would pick me up at noon every day from kindergarten. We'd vanish into the trails. Our go to's were our local Safeway food store. There, we'd sweep tastings and on just about every aisle, as I'm saying this outta "turkey"; Momma musta had known security or somebody cause how we'd eat up a house and home. Although, I am happy and proud of her bravery. I suppose Pop's had a personal interest invested likewise. It shows they did not miss a beep, nor had she and I exploring those tastings. Ham, dry salami, that ol' good turkey outta the packs, and the kind Grannie baked during holidays. "Yeah, those kinds." Had pineapples dressed over the tops, yummy, yummy, yummy! Those visits were as if we held a stock interest in the joint. No question. I'm jaded whether Momma was nickel slick, and or smoother than fresh birth baby's butt cheeks. Wasn't like we were stealing. As Momma always noted, we were only "tasting." Like the rest of the store goers appeared to be doing. Just as subtle. Everybody was in sync, but for sure, our inner spirits knew better. Despite thus, her ways weren't like anybody else's. Which my thoughts would be saying, "You know that stuff in those folks' stores don't belong to you, boy." But I never dared question her actions as a mother. Unlike the other kids, on the other hand, whose parents depended on hoods' babysitters. Lord knows what happens in those situations. I've learned over the years that momma's devotions to local charities were her way of paying honorary for our merchandise tastings. Not saying it's okay to splurge out on the next person's expenses. But she'd caution, "I'm just paying myself a percentage of what's owed us." Now, mind you, our tables and or cabinets on the home front weren't growling. We stayed fully stocked with goods and never went without. Although I often wondered Momma's reasoning for givin' me the name of Maxwell Pixar, but I lived up to it. I'm not questioning any of those decision today. Irrespective, nor the adventurous explore of our plentiful of tastings- quite often. We even hauled along my brother France with us on quite few of our unusual missions. He'd be overly excited after seeing 'lil bro dipped fresher than a pair of the newest Reebok sneakers. But often, he'd blow our disguises. Just the looks he brandished on his facial features yelled, "Please don't think about looking at us 'cause we're outta' bounds!" And sure enough, one day, visibles of ours were fully crept. Mostly happening during one of Momma's other hobbies– racetrack betting, which she forever had niches of favorite picks. How? I do not know to this day, but she was relentless with winners, and plentiful. But leaving France home, now I consider her reasonings. Yet there's times we were forced to take him with us. I mean, he wouldn't surrender and showed out some terribly. Dangerously, he'd chase down the car in middle the traffic dividers in outrageous, crying like someone was tryin' to harm him. As I would vouch to let him tackle alone. Even still, he would make fun of me, whaling, insisting me being of a momma's baby as if the love of hers differed amgust the two of us.

For the first time, I'd admit she was right; her fair warnings of how France was visibly alarming. But it also brought us awareness; having the knowledge we were on the radar had its ups and downs. Yet, I believe still today, as yesterday, leaving him at home wasn't without sufficient merits. He didn't have the same aspects or stomach for the racetrack ramblings. But far from any L-7 (square). He was oldest by uh' few years, although my size was daring, and if we fought, I likely wouldn't ask for seconds, but I wouldn't be upset over the results, I promise you. But our level of respect was well kept. Over the above having a disposition of Momma's. He didn't have to follow with us cause, during shopping, we always included him in our splurging. But it didn't matter; France had to go. That's how he was. But little had he recognized that a quiet spot of side eyed tendencies and prestigious jealousy over his relationship with Grannie had existed.

It was almost divine while vertical how Momma and I moved like a carbon mirror of him and Grannie. France and Grams would get lost in the wind, leaving me at home. Their bond in nature was dynamic of strengths. Just something about that ol' racetrack with Grannie and Momma they loved. But, over the above, it was G'moms who was warped into her some betting. She'd bet our light bill, rent, or any other utilities on the line for her most favorite Jockey-Russel Baze. Often, as I prayed, he'd win, as considering, many of days he'd leave us without lights and in the dark. But it wasn't always that drastic. Majority of the time, Grannie was on her A-game. Boy, she was risky, but she knew how to pick her some winners. Gamma's niche wasn't like none other. Striking big, pulling off pick sixes and trifectas. That's where you'd be cashed out if you hit six races in an orderly fashion or three. Almost like betting the lottery, but there were plenty notable of instances we'd questioned her courage for betting. Still hadn't interfered with any decisions nor desires of her pressings of her luck. "She was never scared" with diligence, shouldn't be viewed through only one lens because some things are life- changing with ripple effects. Therefore, utilizing the better provisions for permutations. I offer holds the volume, opposed to a diagonals gamble approach. The notions of maintaining a slow and steady pace results in the end are greater if you had to determine the values versus the risk, which is only an opinion. They're like assholes; everybody has one. But yeah, we survived off betting for several years, and like anything in life, there are things that do not always come attached to a manual for instructions, but you learn from experiences and push forward. "Have heart, money will follow." Although they are widely spread, glimpsing those options I offer it's like having that winning mentality, a trait you're likely born with, just a perspective vision.

I'm contained momentarily, not on panic mode, as there's a difference between significant quiet dome pleasures and joyousness with a modest type approach, and may hold the actual prones for propensity or may not reflect through the lens of the naked eye. Likewise, footsteps travelled on

Earth, some likely might argue otherwise. But that's where we realize who's on similar wave links with credentials propane like uh' shark can spot uh' diver hundred yards away. As in my sights forever the equivalence of the *valve* having those quartz. Fair to say, Momma had the kinda heart of a tucked olive oil of any phenotype I'd known or learned about, mostly light spoken, cluttered in pain. You've had to have the full knowledge of her silence of innocence. Her breathable luxuries, in hindsight, are today the realities of mines beyond the laws of motion. Her decisions and I flush are like Sprite commercials, fascinating and full of life. Completely, I'm intrigued by her nonresponses to many questions I prompted, but to say the least for her courteous gauges, "forever I'm optimistic– as I'm content." Money is not as difficult to get as it's hard to hold onto. Just saying while learning these luxuries of Momma's, her rhythm is a beautiful quality, knowing how to maneuver under so much pressure. As I opinion, if I ever wanted to revisit the architecture of her designs, required I prioritized with a thorough willingness and to appreciate the facts. It's helped shape the course that I've knitted upon while leaving space for joy in waves of that reciprocal under the silver and murky stripes. "Working smarter, not harder," gathering my thoughts with a sense of ease, anxious to learn from a distance the bravest next steps and adventures of my life's quest. Although making splashes uncompromised along the way as my bro France, who's maintained the unforeseen early upon. How impressive of him.

Chapter 2

THINK OUTSIDE THE BOX

No, I've not discovered the full devotions to the game, but I acknowledge those ultimate concepts of the four levels foundations.

"The gangsta, player, Mack, and hustler." Some women's actions these days have proven and led by positive and efficient examples. To argue otherwise wouldn't do justice for the homage deserved. As a nation, we've progressed over the decades in multitudes in effective ways. Thus, having a strong woman on the forefront, I'll always believe you have greater options, better results with an Intune other half. I notice the outstanding job Pop's musta juggled within character overlaps with bars of a "player and a Mack" as I've discerned portions of actions of his and Mommas. There are real techniques that are too knit- delicate of courtesy as maintained at tender hearts. I flutter the reality as I continue with evolving. Yet mindful while getting money without being penalized versus working under another's discretion. It's a huge difference; the debts hold greater value than moving through life absent any consciences of senses, how women's beauty speak languages which register outta space with us men natural hormones. Far beyond our earth's hypertext data comprehension base. Sometimes, it's very rewardable. As the ability to bind utilizing a single look without per se dialogue. Those qualities are nonpurchaseable, yet they're the finest treasures God provides us humans. Taught via human teachers' school lessons. Those are life options, too kinda inherent you must be lucky enough to prescribe and grasp. It's the whole enchilada. As a youngster, I coulda overlooked those tangibles, but the older I've grown in muster, wisdom sank of a Tiger Woods putts as I'd like to believe. Although the world is reshaping and it's ah good thing right! Further, noticeable trophies are different. As the flavors of Oreo cookies, hard choosing just one; the others are so competitive in taste. Then, it's like the dodge phase of life avoiding those extra calories, almost impossible by our human nature, gotta learn to acknowledge what's effective and their starks.

Tagging under the radar with oldest bro, Dexter. It's whereupon I became clenched with my hustle he'd always recite, "Ah' bar is ah' bar, ah' law is ah' law, uh rule is uh' rule, you must always hold in the purest forms at any given time." Now, what does that symbolize? He'd ensure that, once understood, mastered, and thereof executed, your vision would correspond with mainstream bylaws, and you'll begin upon equating stages. I digested his inferences, noticing. "A Mack is the loneliest guy in the held universe and must get his money without being penalized. He knows that every human person's a threat to his makings, and he's gotta be neat and clean at any given time." Unlike the very characteristic of a player and ah' hustler. Not forgetting the instincts of a gangster, one of the deadly and coldest on planet Earth, who would compromise his generosity to get dough, which conflicted with instances of mine, Uncle Fly's, Pops, and mostly other male figures that I have observed while developing my quest through life. While precedence be, just because you may hold a position or have prospects willing your potentials and thereby assisting those agendas doesn't qualify you nor assign you your identity. I proffer, study the four levels the game recognizes, as it'll likely provide, for those starters, at least that visual roadmap for life's options with its full potential rewards.

Like a sponge, while lampooning, soaking knowledge up, I've happily captured my rubric underneath my own fingernails. What's absent isn't always unquenchable. I harped the sights riding shotgun in Uncle Fly's 1970'ish Lincoln Continental It was cocaine white with suicide doors. No chic of his rode the front seats, but trust anything their hearts desired before even opening their mouths was on deck. He chauffeured and happily insisted, which were varying protocols of his. Not to say his fully shared interests were Prada always. Insinuating anything other, I'd be lying, but the surprising things about it, was outta genuine love. While noticing how they ate, slept, and breathe his perspectives. It became obvious what was germane, how he kept his feet dipped. I'll never forget this one particular babe of his, "BeBe." Ooooh my gosh her thighs were kicking like "you know whose's during the "NFL" halftime game. Those ladies hips in pairs, um! With no extra on it! Whenever she enters a room, to this day, she raises goosebumps on foreheads, as I've found very unintentional. Others' eyes likewise be amazed, clear of wonder. You could sense Unk's loyalties towards her though, mostly any person could. And it showed through features they'd be breathable. Yeah, including women. No doubts! Their panties likely were wetter and moister than an Oakland's merits baked cake. His aims, lazier- fully extended to the highest maneuvers. You were better comparing him to the likes of a "Mayweather" in his prime for measuring his given hustling traits. But they hadn't known they'd learn from a baby of whose vision ranged beyond stock monitories. That's because, for some adults, it's almost impossible to teach anything. They think arrogantly. Us children, who's we for arguing otherwise. But I wouldn't dare backtalk the elders. You'd be ah' fool doing anything differently. And you better not try it with grandparents or Mommas. You'd wanta opt to tongue kissing a light socket risking getting electrified than opening your mouth to differ. Find yourself getting picked off the turf. Aren't you moved with inclinations of the slight thoughts, just shadowboxing their requisitions? "I brought you into this world, and I do not need permission and or shackles to exit you out. Bo-y, don't play with me." As I darted these eyelids her direction, thankfully, she let it slide, leaving me with that silent discipline treatment only.

Without doubt, life during the early 80's had its ups and downs. The fashion industry was mostly known for its platforms, bell bottoms, p-coats, butterfly shirts, and afros. Those were amongst the least you'd expect from the high school turnouts. And if you could bragin your parents into lending you the old school Buick Skylark, duce-in-a-quarter with da' gangsta whites, you were considered uh' Don, which is top-grade boss status. Today's a despair. Our youth appears lost, searching for answers. Yet, still i'm hopeful.

Ever since crack evaded the forefronts, it's put a black eye on the earth's pave and surface. Then, an ounce ran you four to five bands. That's when sixteenths were factors. And if you were working with zones, you were doing exquisite thangs. Not to brag, I've escalated through the rise and destruction of the society we reside. Plus, I've paid my respectful debts, as I hope. Yet, it doesn't make up for our losses or unequal opportunities. But going forward is what's at bay. Each one teaches one and holds the volume prolifics. But it's the unequal disparities I'm opposed of.

While Pops was fully invested in his fair real estate purchasing throughout our entire Bay Area City, his money rock, though, sat on one of the busiest strips in East Oakland. MacArthur Boulevard. "Off the hook." Cracking like nothing seen in a lifetime, like ninety going south where you sent ya' loochie to the front got your bundle out back. Not to whale on the underground trades. But it was monthly one of his fresh whips would slide through the blocks. Ladies would flock nonstop to snap glimps. Then it wasn't any selfies in those days. The world was Kodak, wordplay bubonic; like the lifestyles todate lived. Looking, it's frightening, the reasons for my protest for better ways putting it. Not fully aware then of Pops inference kinda' hampered one's insights from the earlier stages. It's consequences as it's irrefutable despite the naysayers. Requires investing quality time whether climbing mountains or boldly jumping outta flying planes, you must prepare and put in da groundwork for the best results.

Noticing fatherhood obligations, he acted consistently while learning Pops disappearances weren't due to a monkey wrench yet for venturing into public services. The substance of his void absences then I hadn't known until becoming of age. As known, the essentials of a father and son's early relationship stages are very instrumental in one's effectiveness, development, processing, decision-making, and formulation of thoughts, which amazingly is how any person responds to life's hurdles. I contest myself. "You gotta move and bounce, continue progress, or become a zombie." Spread those wings, look beyond, and think outside the box. Don't be content with established unequal playing fields. I've found it quite interesting to explore the experiences of life. There are instances I differ just thinkin' out loud. But if beauty's uh' sin, there's not a reason it's debatable that's drawn.

Chapter 3

LEVELS THE GAME PRESCRIBES

Growing up during the era of the 80s ghetto wars, yes, it's interesting as a child. Our feet stayed moving around the globe. How I managed to grip life skills? That's another story in itself, not a mystery. Nor do I make excuses. You have to admire that innocence holds no grudges. Pops followed his instincts on conquering versus dividing, holding an inner-based bonafide bider's opposition. I wasn't spoon-fed. It was either rap, push packs, or work for bean sprouts! Luckily, the family understood my pains about the distance between brotherhood and fatherhood. It's vivid of its very imprints, a level of the game which we can infer indifferently, but the truth we cannot ignore.

Leaving one to speculate what's condensed, what's on a person's mind genuinely. I would love to drench you with da' historical theories. But I'm not into the slay lions, purifications at any indulgences. Yet mindful of brothers with undivided chains intact, although not raised under the same roofs from the start. The taste of our gutter deep journeys coherently I learned "Off The Dribble" well varied and bedded from the soil. Pop's approach had a bounce, but savvy while introducing us into the rules of life, which I'll imply are the four levels the game subscribes to. "The gangsta. player, Mack, and hustler." Yet there are different levels for each livelihoods. Without quoting him, it's that building of a vision from the grounds up and it forms the structure of entrepreneurship upon you. His purchasing of multiple real estate properties, rehabs, and others were built from his hard labor. As I watched, I learned where fitting in and instrumental was vintage, a mind frame of a hustler. But it's by right to note how my older brother Dexter, under no false pretense, overstood the game and was fluent with admonishments to the streets. I looked upon his path non-diverged and ran with it. Although alone, the ways rerocked certain portions of which only enhances the fundamentals original formulas; in my opinion, others might arguably differ, but inferring there's a lack of diligence, let's let the quest determine, "whether what's outta sight is always outta mind."

Before you knew it, Dex managed to focus on winning whenever Pops wasn't present. Any questions of concerns were placed upon his broad shoulders and instantly followed the answers, not leaving a single bolder unnoticed. Never shown any signs of resistance to acquiring options nor of landmarks, then why must I?

Quickly adapting to the struggles, following the trap rules of conduct without variations nor compromises, we ultimately held our soils' platforms with valid interest. Our hurdles for getting further in life weren't solely based on getting money, but not ignoring the everlasting effects with impacts widely ranged. My brother, underneath the oldest "Network," had the heart to gamble. Brahs' niches for getting money was inconspicuous and phenomenal. But big bra Dex upheld that interest with intuits in tack. While Network, for reasons unexplained, had those human other actions like something outta the Godfathers' playbook, sharp, clean, with major finesse. A smoother pulse, but reflective of Pops at heart grounded on principles just like brothers, we never tried to outshine the other. But once Network acquired his opportunity to floss, the whole Bay Area recognized the differences of his chief's mentality, whose trajectories rang bells worldwide, as groupies were in conflicts of his interest for his boldness. Although, bruh didn't pay it no mind, staying that grounded individual, pushing da' fliest whips, and his tilts (homes) with dough reaching of ceilings. We partied statewide, which at times had its disadvantages, being unlike the others around. I like him; was a loner kinda dude. One woman, and very humbly molded. I modeled those family's traditions, up until the unintended rhetoric with me and my soulmate. In hindsight, we nearly argued our hearts out; who knows the dial, experiences, or the effects of ? It's life you live for the adventures, and thereof the rewards. While somebody's garbage, another person's treasures. My bro France knew how to inbound, although brah Network understood the world quite differently, the dribble aspects, his motto, during lunch hours he'd floss through on the school's radar in one of his various old classic whips. Mustang, Cougars or Chevy's. Mostly sitting on Zeniths and Vogue wire wheels, painted by none other than our hood's famous body paint shop, that be Mr. Garbro himself. But bruh's parade was "extra, extra"! His music was considered our lunchtime recess bells, blasting ridiculously loud, shaking the grounds while skating by doing six miles per hour in a designated thirty-five per hour zone, banggin' the latest hip hop and R&B tunes. His looks hadn't hurt his chances not in the least bit. Without doubts, women were outta their minds over his ghetto persona. Stealing the topic in class at times, over subjects' lessons, lending teachers to often inquire, "Who is this guy captivating and holding my students at attention more so than I am?"

Soon thereafter, Pops began getting the updates of his offsprings. Widely, Network, and big bra Dex, of whose reputations were standing out and drawing heat waves of differences of opinions which superseded Pop's roads of expectations, as our foundations were labored friskin' Pop's responses; as he stepped up his game without any hesitations. To apply equal and satisfying approaches., I myself wasn't into the actual hustling aspects, though visualizing, waiting, while learning my position. What was obvious was unsaid. Staying prepared for the right opportunity, life, as we know it, provides no dog horns or whistles.

Chapter 4

IT'S YOU KNOW OR YOU DON'T

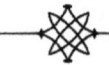

The streets were dancing, and you could sense jealousy amongst the haters bleeding over in our family affairs. The name of ours, Da' Pixars, was ringing louder than the biggest thing since the royal Kennedys days. Network and bra Dex created a vibe which induced stares that was unavoidable, too enthusiastic, establishing a street pulse worldwide. Our revolt held its precedence, which we answered effectively while expanding our logo. My cousin "Mellow", Pops brother's youngest of three sons, put both shoes on the dance stage and made his hoods presence felt, although not at the pace of Network's or Dex, yet it enabled and quick enough to keep the bells ringing. He had the town loving his groves, and his moves were proficient and well in focus with Dex's and Network's. You heard him blocks before seeing his whip miles down the road pushin' dipping through in his four- times blue 70'ish Caprice, old school Chevy, knocking eight fifteen-inch E-V-E's woofers, electronic with crossover amps, Zapco board the Latino homey "Fonzzy" work, super extra dark tents, hubcaps, and elite tires. The streets of Oakland hadn't foreseen nor heard anything like his trophy to date. To his credit, Network, on the other hand, had the block clockwork dancing getten frostbits, cheapest bounce your money could sky, which didn't undermine Cuzzo Mellow's pitch of becoming a legend rightfully in his own lane. Wasn't no time until the other O.Gs were batting in his direction, inferior to his footwork. Yet his posture always positioned him ahead of the game. Of course, he held his ground while up against friction from other rivals. A pioneer breaded into the hustle with a mentality that stood out, well distinguished, routinely kept at least four to five loyal soldiers in distance. Just in case other brands pinched at testing his gangsta.

Network and the other O.Gs on the block opened shop up on what's still known to the town as the first hood's titty bar strip club, which was Oakland's "after hours" spot. Knee deep in the hood trenches, enough leaving other sectors throughout the Bay Area in uproars, willing to go to war over a fair share of the trade's revenues. Ouch! Meanwhile, pole dancing money was pouring, not snoring. This had been in the early nineties. Loot was flowing faster than money counter machines could feed. Never had I seen as many google eyes in my entire lifetime. The beef increased, placing hourglasses in a position of differentiating their potential friendships over money. "You either with me or against me" was drawn. Those efforts worked well for the weeding out the non- synced and the false believers. Unlike how Pops enlisted his footprints, bra, on the other hand, was with da' shit! While

Pop's march was more nonviolent, which is what inched him apart from his competitors. He utilized his energy to build platforms, avoiding the tension and hostility that followed him. He kept a nine-ta-five day job but didn't give any slack, whereas it wasn't just. Mighta been of his upbringing rooted from the deep southern parts of Texas, which founded of a peaceful and humbled stance. But in East Oakland, those days weren't based on reaching happy mediums, although Pops didn't have a Harvard law degree but the underneath sole of his which bogarted such righteous paths. And I muster now, if you don't pay attention to life's detours and hardships, it wouldn't be unlikely for you to lose direction. It happens to the best of mankind. No one's excluded from derails. But it's the bounce back shapes the roads. Best to do a taste of homework. I'm developing, but I'm still at a tender young age, and mind you I'm adapting to the assertions of what's in play, observing and making moves of monumentals inquiring knowledge enabling the lifestyle of four-corner hustling, meaning "getting money without being penalized." As the neighborhoods I've braced sun-up-ta-downs throughout Oak-Town. I do admire yup, but it's no need to state the blocks upon walking distance home to the Oakland A's, Raiders, and the Golden State Warriors, "Yeah, I forewarn you, the area is action-packed!" And in those days, to hang nearby, you were almost obligated to represent the one and only projects. But in the block of which we resided, most of the homies weren't interested in claiming anything other than our turf. We formalized our own clique within, making names for ourselves. "It's you know or you don't." However, the founder of area's district reached worldwide exposure as his infrastructures dipped wide-spread, making him one of the richest, most feared, yet well-respected tycoons on the street level of hustlers. I'll only reference him as "Touchdown" (T.D.) because anytime he handled the rock, our chances of winning soared. His held identity in itself holds vasts- goes without saying bonafide. Statue equivalent to the regards of a prize freedom fighter, but on a revolutionary scale. As I'll only acknowledge him though under "T.D. the General" of the Bay Area, irrespective of the several hoodwinked stories that resulted in numerous federal indictments on and off the benches– leaving more arrests than we'd ever dreamt to have existed. As in honor, excepted by the ways of his wide-open arms moving into the area, I'm paying homage graciously, my momma Margaret, had an opportunity to introduce me throughout the ranks of his. "Town Bittiness" I'm not going to engage upon, nor distort the zones that are not a part of the stated playbook, of which someday likely there are others who may welcome a diagram. For now, I'm only inferring to have understood the rules of power, its foundation to which were designed upon our pave unrooted!

Now, mind you, I'm anointed to the assertions of the hood's quick lifestyles. But it wasn't no time before losing my innocence while dashing out between the danger zones. "Busted!" Kind of woke up a young dude's lane. "Homey," I'm like Whoosh! What in the hell is dat! The first taste rocked a dude's world. Regardless, I'm disengaged with my *sundae* today. For obvious repertoires, I cannot greet it aloud. Although I wished I could, boy I wasn't nearly prepared to introduce another vision to the fields. I played possum from her, my then-secret admirer. Our age gapped perfectly. If you ask me, older women with finesse, tender thighs any day! Forever, I will do my part at every glimpse. To this day, I haven't found the full strength to ask her that million divisidaro's question, like virtue, who's on my radar daily, hiding her boisterous silhouette. Maybe she tore a page outta the four levels, having that hustling mentality, meaning "getting money without being penalized." It's a trait enveloped. Awkward, but it's not only utilized by the opposites. Although it's principle. Yep, I answered the horn! Moody, huh, but I'm hopeful and optimistic, gotta' be because life's real. But I'm mindful. It's never okay to intervene between a person who's in motion getting money.

I'm just posted admiring my precious diamonds. Stay hustling, but guess who's paying attention– daily likewise. Gotta question for you: "Is our world still Jupiter?" Um! What a beautiful sight to behold. You wonder who's jealous of our half the relationship. Yeah, in my b-boys glance, I noticed the effects of the dangers of today. And the global distractions of the real hurdles that are at the forefront, misguiding and feeding our society copious opinions, perpetuating artery spasms. It's obvious that I'm not a neurologist. Yet it's hard to ignore our dense atmosphere, split-pea-crowd. Just doing my part and knot the flossin only offering anti-inflammatory over the latter. Maybe you agree upon the options of solutions. Forfeiting is one thing; defending yourself against the opposition is another. There's a slippery paced slope between the two, with causes and its effects. You're fooling yourself if you thought that generals who formulated the rules of the streets bylaws hadn't debated waivers for protections involving instances that we're living under today. "Ah' quite civil dispute over property rights." Or the likes of, which functions may vary in dynamics yet who's at the debate, a question for the street generals to digest and determine as I'm only inquiring of the nature that appears absent. Although "T.D." Touch Down his void in my beliefs brought uproars, leaving numerous unanswered questions. That being said, while no one thought to study neutrals of confines, what's collectively more a practical matter. Bringing solutions for the difficulties, unlike the reportedly hi-fi-sharp frequencies, which appear incapable of determining our level playing fields under the street rules of hood bylaws.

Known there are erroneous actions, I know of plenty who are currently under wraps for far less. But our society need not get comfortable being blinded upon the rules of unequal fair play from which it's my knowledge the bylaws of equal justice attributes to the four levels permitted on mandates enables the hood generals to amend particulars for the world radiance of *purposes* it upholds and give the oppressed voices, in order to have an effective level playing field we reside under today. As technology advances, the rules and its players must follow suit. Wouldn't you agree there are forms of authenticity that have to be upheld? And because you may hold interest in a tangible substance doesn't give you permission to abuse your potential how one chooses fit. For instances, if you're speeding excessively down highways, wouldn't you be subject to a citation? You must be prepared for those penalties. In life, there are rules and fundamentals that apply to just about anything life has to offer. It's the world's axes. I'ought mind getting acquainted. You.

Chapter 5

FROM THE STREETS TO THE BEEPS

There's differences often questionable requiring of referees, although not to ignore, holding court on the streets or behind closed blinds. But, I offer there's two sides to every glories; gather both before you invoke opinions throwing in the towels and/or alarming referees. We agree to disagree where limitations in participation in upholding our street principles oughta exist. Now, once a person from the hood engages as per se non-negotiable, does the same rules apply to him or her for protecting holding grounds opposing the abrogations of one's personal property and or rights? Not that I have anything in dispute with chains upon commands, in particular. I do honor oaths and positions held. But it's due process I have questions for.

And no, I do not forfeit what's rightfully mine under any pretense of measures. I know the bars. If you mind shadowboxing the agendas, I'ought mind getting in the way. I'm not opposed to good trill, lets us dialogue for abandoning our principles of perspectives. For periodicals, it'll be unperipheral to ignore our fourteen amendments holdings in part:

No state has the right to deprive any person of life, liberty, and or property without due process of equal protection under the law!

Yeah, it's a wide range to inquire upon, moreover, if you exclude those of our peers from engaging in participation. As I balance contentions of intentional unlevelled playing fields. For the latter, we'll wonder the reasons for the subject of non-equality, whether it exists and/or existed, giving these questions aren't gutted inferences. It's an open conversational wound on America's visual fabric. "The actual causes any effects, under the rules of hoods bylaws." Unapprised, it's preposterous, meaning ones outta sync defending against oppressions outta sight, blinded by waivers of due process. Although, I'm hopeful what's of range. Whose jurisdiction upon clarifying our hoods' amendments to which unites ours as it's obvious we've protested, surpassed the kneels, our worlds are beyond viral stages. I do exercise that it's *mindboggling*. May I offer "us" a solution without biases? Probably not. The world's more withdrawn and attentive to any misdiagnosis of our discriminatory quite exclusions. "But okay." Those who are just skating through while what looked upon initial glimpses; maybe someone wasn't on their nickels, instead quarters; at the same time guarding our plates. Attorneys nor judges ought not to have those optional tools of luxuries undermining liabilities upon they've wronged a party, which strikes for a logical debate. Until then, our held society's foundation looks as if we'll be searching while avoiding that which is inhumane. Again, it's only an opinion.

You notice worlds apart divisions, how they wage for differences and behave readily. It's because positions aren't misplaced nor wrongfully abused. And if a vehicle's on the road traveling the wrong direction, whistles are applied required, blown, and honored to the fullest. Alarming, maybe something displaced. Shouldn't take decades for the effects to follow. That's what are referee duties nucleus avoiding tragedies. Like "T.D.," he kept our communities intact, whether you liked or disagreed with approaches applied of his or not. As every ghetto has its hood equalizers, who's dialed into our paves. By virtue holds bylaws in purest standardized forms. You may seek to greet front and center. Even to this day may rise to the highest form of fashions, causing moments of actions. O'well, in my predicate of mind, what's it achieving or acquiring the brow. If you'd ignore, unlearn the styles. Imagine dat; that's the reason you must not assume the answers.

"Let's pivot your personal property is wrongfully obtained during any arrest. Then do you have a right of contesting what's yours?" If you file a timely valid petition, "Yet, aren't you almost obligated to appear or object to those seizures?" This likely requires its principles to engage the oppositions involved, or it'll become forfeited to the stated adversary. Now, are you in violation of the rules claiming ownership rights of what's rightfully yours? "As an American, I believe we are beyond forty acres and a mule," but that's another subject for a broader discussion. But one step further, "If you're wronged in the hands of officials, forms of *unjust*, you file suits against an opposition, its actions to follow. Are you in violation of the street code for wanting compensation? My position is that a person doesn't lose their constitutional rights upon they're violated at the hands of justice on *fighting* back. Others might disagree, but that's for the debate. And it's irrespective of whether the oppositions are of disguise. "Ah' bar is uh' bar, uh' law is law, uh' rules uh' rule, you must be under the purest forms at any given times" if you get blindsided by illegal man down the fields. The hood referees these days appear to have yielded their moral duties and or forfeited the rights upon ours. Whether intentional or if bias in place attached, it doesn't undermine one's position for a healthy resolution. There's a spectrum for protesting stand your ground, or is it not? Again, it doesn't restrain you if a badge comes into an equation. By right, it's circumstances which oughta provide a channel from the streets to the beeps obtaining the rights for exercising due process. "Or is it okay for an opposition to hold a person's momentum from progressions? Instituting only their desires having one-sided predispositions of a person's rights for equal protection? Thus, would who representing him or herself via proper meaning self-defense under the due process doctrines be forfeited, which is granted to *us* American citizens, which is held in part?! And it applies to hood hustlers:

The right to defend him or herself on their own if capable without counsel, under Articles of the United States moving active Constitution. Whereof, my views are a means of treasures good solid ventures and those of pursuance. Unpleasantly, the hood's mentalities have revised our youth's perseverance. Partly, and I do rebuke portions of the brave ridiculousness of ignorance, as it holds no place upon the nests adorabls next in ranks. Those who are out of sync within our world founding fathers' platforms are held required to answer. And I'm not only speaking Abraham Lincoln's. Not that I'm undermining the devotions, but it's our discord of the hood's moral conduct. We as humans, yeah, it's noticeable the difference when not paying dire attention to our established treaties from those domestic or foreign stares.

Might It non-musical to a degree, and then there's *inferences* to be drawn. Nodded and adhered to the differences of opinions, nonchalantly not able to be overlooked, excluded, stolen, and or misplaced without us within exercising better judgment. The world's now on a visual pivotal, obligating these forms of values for obvious reasons, against the joy riders and the unsubstantiated. While of desiring those benefits absent having put in general footwork, some although threatening our mere habitats. But not without conforming with reprimands of neutralization. Risky upon loots involved, you'd be surprised who appears outta thin air. There's nothing wrong with spreading the love, nor am I suggesting arguing any particulars. I'm only given due to diligences of observations." Few kibble and bits don't override obligations of principles. I apologize; the deal runs much deeper than what's between the visual inferences to the indivisibles. And there's nothing wrong reaching across dividers, nor am I suggesting. Unlike supported by diverged thinkers who oppose Civil Unions. Our hoods gotta' be open-minded, permitting revising with our today's evolution. Or otherwise, we'll stagnate, appearing that we are progressing in value, which isn't derisively equal with other cultures' views of the wide world platforms. For if our youth suffers, we've lived in vague, and you've heard the saying, "Taking one step forward and two of backward." It's beyond running in place; we're at a stalemate. Now, we can hold naive assumptions that'll only be self-deceptive of our achievable efforts. Absent exercising blowing of the whistle on violations; of instance, discriminations of racial biases, under equal protection we are living disillusioned. For standards a person must maintain the right to disputes not subjected to others personal opinions, rights, property, fairness against intentional biases, equal responses before forming the exclusions of one's peers, having neutral panel opinions upon meetings of various minds. There's means for reconciling America's retributions involving decades of unfairly grievances of biases, not only towards African Americans. But there exists global unequal treatment on a number set of issues from life's issues attributed to what's playing out right before our very sight. Whether in the streets marching for freedom of expression, contesting a person's innocence, sports events and/or intertwined petit jury biases. Notably, if you haven't envisioned these stages upon your life quest, aren't you from another planet? Imagine any one particular group's insight on any these numbered subjects alone. How wouldn't you suspect not to obtain a biased, one-sided calculated effect? That's knowledge on its visual surfs. Doesn't matter whether it's intentional or a mistake; there has to be level playing fields aside, or the results to follow are nonly- fleeting, with damages that'll surpass decades unforeseen.

Chapter 6

OPPOSITES OFTEN ATTRACT

It wasn't long before crack hit the scene and took our ghettos and city streets underneath its heels. Our whole neighborhoods did three hundred sixty-degree spins. Most got hooked and strung out on drugs. Handwritten, grimmies, a.k.a. mouth shutters, lasers, playboys. Had stomachs doing things you never dreamt, farting, cartwheeling, and leaving the homey's checking drawers and undergarments for the wreckages. That's how potent and raw it was. In no time, the nation caught a glimpse, reprogrammed our global vision. Had back pockets touching.

The neighborhoods got ugly drugs, gang fights you name it. My Mom and Pops, in particular, were fed up chancing, wondering if one day their baby wouldn't survive another day. They decided it was worthy a visit down south, Houston, Texas, to distant family, and I hesitantly agreed. Boy, it was rough leaving the lifestyle that I'd grown used to. And just getting my feet wet. Although it wasn't forced, still was as if I didn't have any other alternatives, almost like a conspiracy. But I followed their advice and hauled myself and my two bags, traveling by Greyhound bus, which took us forever to get to Texas. But looking back now, if only I'd known the differences between being desegregated from the surroundings of the exploding drug scenes of the early eighties. Of course, yeah, I missed the homeboy-triage state. Not trying to ridicule, but I never woulda batted even uh' lid. Country living wasn't anything I'd foreseen. The trip sufficed as though the journey we were on was gonna be a lifetime vice grip. We stopped at least seven times per day for food, snack breaks, gas, and picking up passengers. For more than half of our trip, imagine who stayed zoning off that ol' Cali good- good underground far beyond any musical raves.

Dipping through different states was refreshing, to say the least, well refurbishing, meeting multiple flavors that represented other perks and paths of life. In particular, this one piece, "Golden Day", who was from Louisiana. Our encounter came during my route to Texas. Although she had me age-wise, so what! Betcha' game was heavily spit. I found the gap between our age differences to our benefits. Utilizing the alike language we spoke towards our leisure benefits bridging barriers of our understandings. Without any verbal's involved evoked laughter. For a second, I thought something was hay-wired, unattractive of how I appeared and spoke. Then I realized it was my Bay Area swagger that had her ticking like a time bomb, from how she couldn't keep still.

The sun was fading, signaling it was getting late. Golden spoke the waiver for germinating. "What you about to do?" That's the only thing sunk in my mind. The tight suspense was at its highest level of magnitude. It appeared her mind was already made up. I wasn't near protesting. I quietly leaned into my seat, observing the four levels, idling her pace. She calmly waited until the entire bus went asleep, and then she began making her moves precisely, not missing her target. I managed an appetite of mines, almost incapable of sustaining. My initial probes, I kinda may have appeared a little bit nervous "yet" fully in tune, as i withheld unfolding my intentions. I laid in the luffs off the radars visualizing what Uncle Fly just beforehand deduced me. Letting nature lead its own course, which is often known as the keys to virtue. Simply relax. As I gazed upwards, and before you knew it, she had repositioned herself into my lap. "Just like that!" Making her way at home plate, raising others' interest peeking in our direction, while awaking the guy seated right behind, like two aisles over, forcing her to stop entertaining. Was I heated.? Pissed off, you bet. I'm like, damn! "What you playing for?" As Golden pleaded and begged that I hold the noise down, I applied my best behavior.

Now, mind you, she'd given me her full identity and her destination. I impressed questions upon myself, "This gotta be one or two things." A Narco or a hell-of-a-money trap. I proceeded, opting the latter gotta be the biscuits. No decoy wouldn't have stirred in and outta lanes offering samples without doubts first. My instincts were not to go for the bait, Max, I immediately calibered utilizing brain power forbidden-triggered optimism. Before noticing, she had my thoughts out on the surfs and in check, which meant, "Greedy, you must not fumble and move lethal!" She wasn't for barter, which she insisted her only contentions were of makin' me smile. Her moves were unlike any I've seen to date. She controlled my no's and yes's. I'm like OK! Let's reverse this: getting this money without being penalized was always the first intentions. Differentiating the two-headed objectives, I alerted myself. "Max, look whatever you do, stay at the assignment." Still not denying her ways of the likes of a golden medal goddess. Fascinating in her own fruition. She had that, you know, gift that kept on giving. Things about her they spoke unbothered to the soul of mine, which sparked out loud. "I know you understand this game way more than just money." I'm like, damn! Bet, fasho we on da right gaps! Rudely interrupted mid-faze by some dude seated right behind the two of us. Initiated with letting out his loudest yarns, insinuating. "I'm not asleep, I'm wide uh' woke." Though, I fought the hardest to ignore what was about to become a mysterious disturbance, which prompted her to insist. "You have to be quieter, Max." Yet her actions held me against my will. Placing a young man's thoughts, traveling a million dialects per second. Fearlessly,

I bounced up and darted into the buses bathroom to regroup my better judgments. As my bites returned, they were vertical, finding the right combating jabs, leaving her awed, unspoken with enthusiasm, dashing– but pumping like a Texas oil well.

I wasn't against her leaps of joy. In fact, right up front, let it be known, "You've got your hands full, lil' momma." But not overplaying the situation. I held off from conveying my inner perspectives of expectations underneath my breath. I hinted satisfaction was evidently another level she had to earn. Wasn't gonna be given freely. Yearning within for an equal pleasurable response of return. Noticing competition was on the boards, testing my qualifications, I wasn't in the least aspects moved. "You know money, it doesn't come with instructions." I forewarned her. Applying the rules, I'm driving this 'Harley', no ghost ridding the bars or compromising my position. I baited.

You know there's winners and losers in every game of life. "So, which angle are you objecting to be positioned?" Golden blushed before responding, "Hickory and in the finest deserts." Barbeque! Wasn't what I expected from her. I'm like, whoa! Where'd she find those tasty thoughts? You know Max wasn't against peeling her outta those seams but kept my attributes platonic. As opposites often attract, they'd latched. Seizing da' moments, not letting the opportunity slip between the gaps. At the same time, both of us unleashed, awakening the other pedestrians on the bus, talking about discomfort. No, I doubt that! We splurged. 'What' we shouldn't have." Instead, we owned our prones. As the spectators hawked from distances in disbelief at our magnifying wavelengths, both in full-fledged. Our lifestyles reflected one another's—the struggles, ups and downs, rounds and rounds. Giving the rules primarily dealing with women are known to nature, they're overly protective of their hearts. It's those held imbedded views we chimed upon mostly while preparing to go our different ways. Our departure configured unspoken obligations captured by genuine wettest kisses. It's then I passionately discovered my unanswered questions upon which my life's journey was defined upon. "If silence couldn't speak, effects wouldn't blush." Every step taken from there on has propelled me forward towards victory, unfolding before the very eyes upon mine. Wrapped into her fatal vulnerabilities. But damn! Those actions of hers, whoa! They were relentlessly too much outta the unethical for obtaining total silence. But, it wasn't because I hadn't given my best decrees at the same noticeables. The buses and other pedestrians deserved mutual respect. As I held heaven from slipping too far away, the dude seated a couple of spaces over prompted.

"I apologize, sir, but if you need any assistance, let me know." I almost thought Golden Day was utilizing me floating interest from the other google eyes positioned strained on her. Her responses hadn't suggested otherwise, nor enticed of opposite; yet instead, only bolstered the consistency of my impressions from her initial first swipes. Indeed, she was about that hustler's lifestyle just as surest money exchanges hands.

"Listen, old man, you do not know me like dat. Watch yourself this enter to win, like Lotto, you know the routine." Owe! That sound bite rocked louder than an Oakland A's sports arena crowd as I couldn't believe what was kicking up outta her smart box. But like new money, Golden's response yelled out at its own mirror for in itself. She and I found it rewarding to make the restroom a tentative getaway. Outta sight, but not outta mind. As I pretended, none of the others were paying attention, uninvested with no strings attached. Shame on me, right, huh? It went on fine, worked out until the rage of Golden's crying out diamonds had increased as other adventurous mentals began peering, notably the guy seated behind ours. Playboy space was ghosted. The rest of the spectators were caught off guard, posting up near the buses bathroom like at a stadium's arena half-time game interlude. Everybody whom spectated had smiles on their facial features upon she'd returned, including myself, which appeared an hour, maybe probably nearly forty-five-the longest minutes.

Looking overly exhausted but well satisfied. I coulda' sworn she ran uh' marathon. I asked her if she lost or misplaced anything. Her nevermore attitude was unable to fully effectively survey how perfectly our moods aligned. But she proceeded like there was nothing to question. I wasn't arguing; she dipped out there assuring.

"I've not had better despite our pulling a disappearing act!" Inferring maybe her absence deserved its own theories, not up for the debates, likely consisting of a myriad set of topics that would soon maybe have to be considered presumably.

"Greedy."

"Yeah, I fired out quickly," which she assertively addressed me by. I instantly looked with a sense of urgency and attention. Like what's popping, wishing I'd mastered the whole four levels the game of life prescribes, yet contained like the youngest most luckiest in the worlds universe, besides only partly imposed, but enough know how to keep my focus from going astray. Once we exited the bus in downtown "Houston, Texas." More unfolded than i expected. She reached her hand in my sweatpants' pockets and placed her phone number written on a piece of napkin, leaving me $360-something in coins. Without doubt nor words, it had the young boy shook! Although, I never let it show. But a player had been suddenly born right on the spot. It was no looking opposite when we departed the bus. It was 110° humidity scorching heat. I almost like ta' died. You know I've never seen up close skin color on folks that was as dark and beautifully lovely as black licorice, and there to retrieve and pick me up. It was my grandparents and my father's three brothers. We hugged, made light conversation, and then fluttered into the Texas wind. Wells, my father's youngest brother and I looked like identical twins and acted alike. You knew we were about to get lost in traffic and cause static. Pop's personality musta rinsed off on him, as too surprisingly, we both loved similar hustles. His niches were raising bulldogs, cows and growing farm crops. For a country boy, it wasn't bad, considering.

During our trip outta town to our final destination home, whenever I even thought of utilizing any improper sentences, Grannie quickly was correcting my vocabulary's grammar. I knew, boy, it was about to be a miserable vacation. My Bay Area dialect was like a foreign language from another planet. Even though we'd yet arrived at the house, dang! I was already to do uh' full revamp headed back to Oakland, but instead, I made the best of my whereabouts. Further knowing, it was impossible otherwise anything other as I made the situation Jade. But it wasn't simple coming from a city lifestyle that hardly slept, which required a different mindset outside of Mercedes and Auston Martin's, to make imaginary adjustments.

There weren't any street lamps, nor hang out kicking it spots. Our fun time was riding horses, fishing, hunting while lunching parties around the barn. Although I browed, which didn't help one bit, we were forced with school riding the yellow buses, which was never anything I wanted to get used to but was compromised and perplexed. In Cali, at home, those forms of transportation were reserved for the, you know, which differed apart from my bounce. But Grannie was real old-fashioned in her ways; she didn't ask anybody to do anything more than once. And you'd be a fool to suggest or refuse otherwise. She upheld zero talk-back rules in full effect. Like the three knockdown standards during a boxing ring match. Felt tantalizing how she'd enforce her orders and effectively with non-tolerance for bullshit. That southern real non-forgettable love was G-Ma stock regulations. Grandpa, on the other hand, you had better luck. He was kinda' more lenient, not much, but you had better action sliding. Pops wasn't stressing on anything much other than his income revenues proceeds circulating from his field of cattle, and it was plentiful!

Chapter 7

ALIHT DAT PART

After convincing myself that I wasn't leaving Texas anytime soon within the next year, well, it wasn't too bad. Just smelling those ol' mules farting up storms, which drove the hell outta me crazy. Didn't make no sense for the atmosphere to have stunk like that. Damn! As everybody knew everybody, the town was knit tight, which was uh' good thing. Had you needed any assistance, it wasn't far. I played sports for our high school team during my freshman year. Making the starting middle linebacker's position number fifty-two. They referred to me, "Number one, bite that dust." Leading in tackles and interceptions. Plus, earning the defensive player year's award had the local chicks lovin' me outta this world, which was my best reward for such dedication. I worked and played hard, yet smart. Kept an above GPA grade average standard of 3.7 on and off the field, was ah' cold piece of work, women rode tough– nonstop in every which way but loose.

Fast forward a year later, after multitasking, I'm having visions of leaving the south, dancing through Oakland with big bro Dex and Network while posted shotgun, giving older women rice looks. Uh' young player was beyond sniffin' mules farting, picking watermelons, and making cane syrup. Although it was fun, you know, the old rituals though, "I love you, but I gotta go." Yeah, dat part!

Ah' dude needed a saddle for of enabling the strapping down at times. It was on thick, but I loved the traffic. Uh' young Mr. Weather boy, with experience. Kinda still wondering how I didn't go pro. My body and mind wasn't on that field in particular, but I'd have ta' apologize. They didn't make enough for the whoopings and bruises. Leaving my thoughts at the time primarily set, "How am I about to be getting back on California's radars." I have to nerve that living under the Texas livelihoods revealed to me something that I hadn't known much about. Discipline, which is worthwhile recommending for any youth growing up in lanes that I once floated within. Uncle Bubba, my Pops, other brothers who's feisty and aggressive as ever and very seldom traveled off the roads. Yeah, but ol' Grannie required me to be duteous, supervisions. There wasn't much chance of making any moves further than her borders. It was nondurable. Not on her watch. What you thought, you certainly weren't about to be ridin' no mules busting no moves! But then again, that mighta did the due. Unlike East Oakland, where every corner was uh' knot spot. What don't we under grasp about the four levels and rules for proper performances which requires a proper mindset enabling the sought results? Maintaining flexibility only enhances for a maximum productivity 'cause hittin' that gravel hard for twelve of the damnedest months was rough to travel. By the end of high school year dipped around, I couldn't wait to have made above-average grades, which opened prospects of returning to my Oakland stompin' grounds. The off-da-hook summertime festivities with sideshows, where D-Boyz brought out their latest trophies and not wifey's and spun until our tires burst into flames. The skating rink in San Leandro was ideal and nothing to sleep on. You found us leaning, and I couldn't wait. Meanwhile reflecting, Uncle Bubba, my pop's other brother who's feisty and aggressive as ever and very seldom traveled off the roads, but if you thought he wasn't watching, you had better thought again. Anybody but Unk! If you ever wanted to know what was moving N- grooving around the barn, you were welcome upon to inquire. But not with Uncle Bubba. If you insisted, he'd care less. He'll leave you with the exact thirsty response every single time. Didn't matter the subject or the substance. You knew his answers to follow, which was always "T'ought know." He'd look you right in the eye, giving you this unmatchable grin, saying, "Like for real, I'ought know. That's to anything, anybody asked him, and be gangster serious, it was routine" to anything– anybody asked him, even before getting ah' response out, you already knew his feedbacks. That's what I loved about Unk. He'd know the answer you're huntin' and then swear up and down. "I'ought know." Say like Granny's in her bedroom, now let's not forget that we resided in a three-bedroom flat. The dining room and kitchen open into our living room corridor areas. Leaving only the bed and bathrooms outta sight. And I'm just gettin' outta school dippin' into the house one day asking Unk like. "Where's Grannie at?" Unk looks me right in the eyes and says, "I'ought know." I'm like, you don't know! What you mean you don't know? I'm like you haven't darted outta the house the entire day." You'd think Unk was back in East Oakland running bundles and being questioned by OPD (Oakland Police Department) or a knock drug scorer. But surveillance conscious was just the way he rocked. I could give uh' damn who asked him anything. The exact response was known forthcoming, holding his fancy grin "I'ought know." I'm like for real, Unk! That was da' funniest shit. Uncle Bubba, Uncle Bubba, Uncle Bubba!

Boy, it was the longest year I've ever lived, naw! It wasn't I'm lying. 'But it hadn't completely zoomed by, but I enjoyed those southern grassroots. Departing was much tougher than the arrival. It's because you know how grandparents bonded love be.

Chapter 8

GONE WITH DA' BLOWS OF WIND

On the route back to Oakland, the gutta' thoughts of getting money had me nervous. I knew I hadn't lost the lust for the love of money in a years' time. I could sense the gifts revisiting before the plane grazed the runways. Thinking about getting blitz and pushing up flossin' in dope fiend rental whips. It's what we did, you know it, hanging, bagging in the four-level bathing's, the whole grand slam. It was like a dream once the loudspeaker of da' Pilot announced. "Listen, passengers and my helpful flight attendants, buckle time for safety. We've got roughly 15 traveling minutes before landing. We're nearing Oakland's base" The relief was in itself a disturbance from the turbulence and knowing Im about to be getting my feet wet again. Those ol' thoughts of what Oakland had manifested within a year's time skyrocketed the level of my anxiety off the scales! Managing the notion of having to refocus was joyful. But I wasn't much able to hold a decent conversation. Every spoonful of spoken words revealed the taste of love as if drinking a cold *Sunkist* on a summer afternoon. Yet, finding the very potential of expanding on my hustle from southern roots into the Bay Area had my whiskers attuned. As I'm exiting down the airport's jetty, Momma yelled out. "Babe, look where you looking– I'm not over there." As I dashed into her arms, the very first thing she asked, "Hon-ey, what in the heck they been feeding you, boy?" I assured. I wasn't late nor ignorin' any meals.

"Good ol' pork chops, muster greens, home-fried potatoes, cornbread, and black-eyed peas." And yeah, I can't let you forget Granny's tasty southern home-style chicken and dumplings." Look-it-you, dang! You-put-on-some-pounds." In her Tamar Braxton noticeable soundbite, as I peered nearly unrecognizable; plus, it hadn't hurt me to pick up a down south drawl, but it was easily detectable. You know how a person extends certain phrases, right! That's what I'd gravitated to, maybe just the indifferently things about myself spoke out. Not on purpose yet, not discarding the roots. But it was something about being from down south, was like the whiffs of fresh air.

"Where's grandma, France, and the rest of the family?" I quizzed Momma upon en route. "They're at the racetrack as usual, but don't quote that for sure. Besides, you know I don't be pealing up in people's business. I just do me. That's how you live beyond your youth." Yep, and under the radar boo-lo-solo." As I thought to myself, Momma drove towards the hills on Hegenberger Drive. There had to have been a sports event at the Oracle Arena that day because traffic was backed redundantly up. It's often like that when our Oakland Raiders have home games. Nothing against the A's. But that ol' Plunkett he knew how to fetch that leather, didn't he? But I wasn't focused on any games, not today. The only game on my mind was the game of life, and mastering the four levels better positioned myself if propositioned again like the ride to Texas had presented itself, brushing up against another Golden Day. Whereas I dove blindly, despite our age differences, I wasn't willfully comfortable relinquishing the keys to the whip, not so quickly. But something about her amused the fuck outta me! Had me debating tracking her down to inquire whether or not she was reluctant to visit the Bay Area. I knew it was a steep leap, but dismay wasn't being superstitious of my conquest. I began reasoning in mind.

Now I'm home, which was like Las Vegas. Our city hardly slept. "Dexter," vigorously having conquered each of the four levels the game subscribes, he knew how best to apply moves which vaguely resulted in the next level of victories on the other side of the game that business conjures for prospering, of which worked out daily at my mental traits.

Upon pulling into the driveway at Granny's, the block sightings instantly brought chills within. The hood homies were out posted around the storefront. I quickly noticed how much hadn't changed except for maybe the few paint jobs on a couple drop tops and old-school hoopties. A couple new faces out there holding the bag, at least that's how I perceived it at initial glances.

I assumed everybody was down with da' politics, fresh prospects included, and itching to earn uh' strip or two, but they wasn't about to get none off me. You know my lifestyle these days. My hustle had its own instructions: "Off the Dribble." If you ask me, they appeared headed in the wrong direction, and I wasn't interested in following those whipz. Nope, surest hell didn't have any interest. But I kinda wondered whose bundles they mighta been toting. They looked hungry how they was running up and drilling the knocks. But I thought, they fasho better keep distances of me cause soonest the L'Roy's push, you knowin' they throwin' that shit nearest whomever closest.

Before even finishing uh' sentence there goes taskforce hitting our block. "Just like that! What in the world do those bum ol' weirdos do as predictable? This ol" bum threw his shit right on the ground near my feet. "Put your hands up, put your hands up!" Trees was everywhere! Scattered out on the pave. Five or more six-foot plain clothes hillbillies with pistols drawn waiving at us like something fresh off a rodeo cowboy flick, pushing our limbs in the dirt. Momma screaming at the top of her lungs. "Please don't shoot my baby! Please, officer, he hasn't done anything." I knew I hadn't. Although scared outta' my draws. As they swore, the work found on the grounds pave belonged to me. How in the world is this happening? I've not even gone into the house yet and am already about to get lampoon (arrested). But not if Momma had any say. As I gazed forward, another unmarked patrol vehicle was dipping up, and exiting out of the rear was a slender white older gent, approximately thirty'ish, whom I noticed appeared was undercover. Insisting I purchased something right upon our arrival as we pulled into the house driveway. The officer implied. Causing Momma to lose her marbles. "Bullshit! You've never seen him before, not uh' day in your life. Look, he's only gotten off the airplane an hour ago, returning from Texas. His plane receipt is in my purse. Look, I just picked him up." Relinquish the officer my ticket. But it was quite obvious they had performed their opinions already. Yet, it hadn't stopped Momma's campaign; she was fully animated over activead ready for war!

"Further, he's only a teenager." Momma impinged my defense relentlessly, which was obviously disturbing to the O.P.D.'s as they gathered into a huddle, rubbing their heads like, You know, maybe we've gotten this one wrong! But it did little phasing how Moms vigorously argued her held position, just uh' braking on, like it wasn't no tomorrow, and she wouldn't quit.

"You know what, just let me get your badge numbers. I know how to handle this. You won't be out here harassing mines no more. This much, I promise you." She let loose fully cans of whoop azz on those plain clothes. Thank God she hadn't gone inside when we first hit the block; otherwise, likely that ordeal could have gotten really ugly and quickly. But they didn't want no smoke outta Moms. The entire neighborhood came out partaking in our defense. Snapping photos, you know, the typical. Back in those days, we didn't have cell phones for instant flicks, only camera devices then. Soonest you took the photo it slid out front, leaving you swaying your arms for it to fully develop as it dried. Man, I looked around, and the other two homies boned out who were posted musta been on the grind. Shit, I coulda sworn lighting struck. How quick they was outta there. Gone wit' da' blows of wind. Couldn't even describe those Nikes. We finished and headed into the house, but she wasn't letting up. Momma had her full-fledged foot on the gas, not giving a break. Now, here's Grannie. Oh, my Lord! I knew it was about to get drastic. She pounces into the ruckus and yells everything outta the book to the L-roys. As the final words she disbursed were, "You wait until I'm finished with you!" But it wasn't as how much of what she yelled. It's how she landed the vipes on her every uttered words. You just assumed she had something other cooking underneath her intentions.

Chapter 9

ASPECTS OF LIFE

Meanwhile, nothing hindered our housewarming party's events. The vibe was notably electric right as I'm darting through the front door. It was on like Fox News Debates. My aunts, uncles, their kids, a host of friends jam-packed our three-bedroom ghetto flat. We were stacked like sardines. And they had the nerve arranging to have had my first hood crush from outta middle school lodging in the house, whom I'd given my first kiss to. Her name was Kim. Not that one. But I gotta say, it was nowhere near France's parade. Brah was doing the fool, him and his tight eyes, who visibly appeared to have had a mighty good interesting understanding' going on over in their own sidebar. One could sniff their vitals, and it was bacon scented, the ol' Applewood smoked flavor, the kind that comes in the open and shut containers. I interrupted the opening with a humorous dialogue approach. I questioned his "Max Juline" sti-low from Tha Mack 70's flick. France's whites lit up brightly giving off that signature glare which imposed money motivated his grit, forewarnin' lil bruh; you better get wise and smell what's on the stove, breakfast bra-brah you ain't knowing. As if I committed a crime during broad daylight, questioning his reasoning on flossing so hard, him and his exotic work, how they strutted the tiles. As this was quite unfamiliar territory that he'd brought out such a mystique arm piece, for a supposedly private family's affair. But it was mindfully innocent as his philosophy for introducing lil bra', it mapped out. I'm like, "Where's Lil Momma's twin friend?" She was caught off guard. "Oops! Next time, don't worry, I'll not forget you, Max." I waged my response. "And I'mm hold you to it, quit playing." I assured her my realness wasn't for play and not to get my Texas vacation years of kindness confused with getting it "OTD." The same rules applied!

Meanwhile, at home on the forefronts, primarily bro "France" was racking in the dough holding down the fort. His quadrilateral moves were keenly grandfathered in the running with our hood's generals and one of T.D.'s knit favorable soldiers. It wasn't long before others around the area noticed his footsteps, as noted. Upon I veered opposite the streets, not deterring my goals to engage with other paths, more creative ventures of life, which consisted of hustling getting off printed merchandise at sporting events, within distance on feet to which we resided. Pushing out T-shirts and other paraphernalia, the opening and closure aspects of the game, which came first nature to us! It was booming! Realizing today, it's likely never gonna be quite the same how dudes nowadays getting money. Because it appears absent instructions, leaving our next of breeds drowsy, not following suit, unfine tuned-blinded of principles, and if abandoned, it's obvious bridges built over decades will suffer. Meaning without guidance, there's unpredictable hardships, no ambiguous thoughts for others who'll make excuses. But the turf we excelled, while splurging with integrity, meaning we offered that symbolized approach, the opening and closure aspects of the game, which came first nature "OTD" to us! While still forming other subsidiaries within other districts, at the same value, acknowledging rules of principles and the dangers with an opened mindset of humility and nascence's not deviating, balancing upon the differences of opinions and personalities. We lived determined to formulate our held positions on historic boards. Neighborhood spotlights. Toe to toe, blow fa' blow even today, not much has changed other than the Zodiac's of authenticities. But it's at times, footworks aren't discernable, at least not under the naked visuals, though the effects are blatantly utilitarian. Representing, we're not subjective to anything other than what's rightfully due, which fa' score, learning one's position is like a science project chasing a goal in its purest form of art. It's heart felt as "Uh 'bar is uh 'bar, uh 'law is uh law, uh 'rules uh 'rule, you must be receptive of the purest forms at any given times for proper define recourses."

Chapter 10

GHETTO LIFE BYLAWS

For the next several months, getting my life on track was an experiment which fluctuated in phases like an uncorrelated graphed plot. From hustling to enjoyment of my own supply, which is rule number one of vividest violations despite getting loot mighta came easily attainable. The difference in my orients focus was in the diaphragm unlinked towards any economics, of prosperity, stagnations in my quest upon life's outlooks, another level that I wasn't quite dialed then to handle, for answering modern-day cash routes today. Maybe to much weed smoke was drainin' my momentums. Things I once enjoyed was like shadowboxing with an invisible person until reality had settled and pushed itself aboard. Then, the hurdles decreased, and my conflicting attitudes were rendered within. I vowed to grapple with my spiritual threads, never to surrender my purpose. No, of course not. It wasn't always tasteful, but the efforts were healthy and humane, though the adventures of tugga-wars existed, and inflamed by improvisions of an executrix appearing counter of my life's daily goals, holding her own stance which was ordinarily questionable to a degree. But it offered not many slight variations of the four levels which often I've been non-repellent of, not that it blindsided me, nor do I subsume to have applied truancy responses yet, I'm just admiring at distances. Trust there's nothing

I adore other than. Noticing provisions of how far we'd proceeded. I could only uphold that bedded certain amounts of dignity while staying focused ahead. At home on the forefront with my arm piece deciding my next money moves. My phone rang, and it was from Victoria. A notch outta the hood, inquiring. But I didn't answer, not purposely ignoring her, but it was beyond bedtime kinda late, and you know us folks, it's difficult to function off alcohol. I maybe had uh' few too much to sip, but often we wanna' believe otherwise. Knowing too much Patron invites that optional for uh' surprise to dip through. But rarely stops the drink circulations. We don't listen. And before you know it, the dance floor starts getting mushy, elbows flying, folks wanna get their shine on grooving busting uh' move, electric sliding, liquor get ta' spilling everywhere, and then it's mutha fu this, mutha fu that, folks airing out decades of old grievances, and I.O.U's and so forth. It's hard at times to congregate amongst our fambam, some. And if free drinks gets involved, forget any civil unions.

Just sayin' no offense. We show up and out. It's no illusion, cause that's just what we do good! I've learned to live with it. I've heard even at some family events requiring metal detectors and security. Now that's just too damn ghetto! Let's not go there. Like yesterday's gatherings resulted in too much drama.

Grandpa yelled out, "Cut it out before I getta kicking ass until it rope like okra up in here!" Sounding like the homey DMX. That's just the ways of his and stock amongst our fambam. You'd almost heard uh' pen drop afterward. It got so quiet after Pops finished his growl. But with Momma, it gets way more exquisitely; too quiet. That's whenever she's on the radar fronts, it doesn't matter who's on stage, they taking a back seated position. Those are the formats I've only known and grown to adjust. It's a routine bylaw within most ghettos, "Grannies are the boss of the bosses."

The next morning, it was rise and shine. You smelled those smothered homestyle fried potatoes, rice with onions, almost impossible to avoiding dippings. You found the entire house dancing through snagging early bites, getting caught loose, and Grannie screaming out. "Get out of those dishes, and out the kitchen! It's not time to eat yet! People dropped butter biscuits, then dashing into the colsest restroom pulling in place as Auntie Donna prepared breakfast. You knew if she was cooking, it was almost guaranteed consensus who's running the floor. It belonged to her and not uh' soul to be within ten yards of radius while she's doing her thizzal. Anyhow, meals on wheels better count me. Run it. There's nothing like a good ol' home Saturday buffet gathering with da' fam. And on this particular day, we're engaged at the table with intriguing dialogue, which kinda didn't involve anybody honestly besides Grannie and Auntie Donna. Myself just being noisy.

Sounded extra classified, as always. And they didn't want me listening in, ordered that I go find myself some business. Sent me to the store to pick up a pint of pet milk and ah' jar of Hometown Coffee. Upon I made my way without further questioning, just as I'm leaving outta the grocery mart, I noticed the same group of Police who stopped and frisked on me just the other day. Upon I'm approaching the exit, they yelled.

"Stop right there, put your hands above your head, don't move, you're under arrest!" Outta nowhere, slapping those restraints on my wrist so tight, biting like a Talk Show host's hips. "We've got a warrant for your arrest." Now I'm looking like where are we going wit' dis. knowing I hadn't done anything possibly wrong. It had to been uh' mistake, they'll get this right; don't panic, which is predominately easier said than done, but it's how you handle vigor any instances of fishing expeditions of those when you have limited elbow room.

"What am I under arrest for, officer?" I barked.

"This thristy District Attorney has filed what's known as a secret Indictment for possession of controlled substances."

"What! An indictment. I almost lost my mind. Before you knew it, I'm hauled into downtown, thrown into the hood's patty wagon, and booked on rigged charges. I thought I wouldn't be able to post-bond because of the age variances there was no way out. Instead, I provided an alias, everything spiking my age, in hopes of increasing any chances of bonding out. Must I note, I hadn't experienced adult jail in the past, but I'd watched more T.V. than enough, enabling how to make it out alive. The first and most important thing, do not interfere with other people's bitness, which isn't a rule unkept!

Soonest we arrived at the station, I asked to use the horn to dial Momma. As they had refused my request to speak with my attorney. Implying, we'll get to that once you're fully booked. They stripped me out of boxer underwear. As I protested, the officer signaled to his group of buddies. "We got one!" His persona didn't appear the least bit concerned with my welfare. But I followed his orders, not putting up any tussles. It's known hardheads make uh' softer cushion. I wouldn't disagree, nor was I interested in finding out.

Seventy-two hours went by like uh' high speed. I'm booked now into a holding unit known as "The Broadway Seventh Building." It's da' worst of worstest, and the biggest test of my detention, twenty-three and one locked away, was how we spent our days confined. Starring out the windows, counting passersby vehicles on the on-street highways. If you were lucky to have gotten a room on the street views, otherwise, you'd pretty much was looking out the windows at the rocks, biting your nails; thinking I done screwed the f_up! Not then realizing the last of precious innocence were under decline statuses, leaving me over indispensable of the lost moments. As the days skied quicker than they'd arrived. I felt derailed from a lifestyle unforgettable by the tilted smiles which yelled through unspoken facial features. My griefs and pains are unmatchable, the reciprocal frames even though the lights were out, still genuinely spoke uh' language in tongues. "What in the world you've gotten yourself into now?"

Thirty days later. "Mr. Max Aswad Pixar, grab your property."

"You're leaving."

"Where am I headed?" I tentatively asked the jailer, leaving my fears and ambitions at once switching places. Yet the deputy receded with uh. "Why. You need something?" not hardly expecting an answer. Nor had I provided any.

"To Santa Rita Grey blocks, full of young gladiators like yourself." Into the wagon we dipped, slidin' through the traffic. During the ride, there was total silence, at least on my part. But the other guys engaged of bragging conversations about their neighborhood sections getting put on different sets by the older foot-ranked soldiers. I laid my marks back on Seventh and Q-Broadway. Dudes wasn't making no noise on getting no money, wasn't energizing the brights of Maxwell's. I posted minding mines. But I found the time to exchange Google stares with a super fly superb lil momie who pulled beside the transportation vessel, who couldn't keep her eyes on the road, was reckless eye borrowings; doing more swerving in and outta lanes, pushing her lil drop convertible starch white, VW Jetta. Making her maneuvers, obvious only inspired my likelihoods of becoming active sooner than expected. We utilized hand signals, had me attuned to finding prize possessions offering fully nonverbal dialogues, but well enough for discerning her phone digits and more.

I yelled, getting the ol' officer's undivided attention.

"Aye, homey slow up some, let lil baby catch up driving the white Jetta." Dude was drunk or too much enjoying himself, he had nerves.

"If you not holding out got you covered." He knew good'n well, I wasn't rocking like dat. But I wasn't about to throw it out there for what. I repositioned our convo "you know three's a crowd, quit. I'm aliiht!" That response kinda' ruffled those feathers as it silenced the whole vehicle.

"Quiet guys, no more talking the rest of the ride." You know I wasn't much bothered! Plays on lil' momma hadn't required anything other than eye contacts and hand motions anyhow. "Wait uh' minute," she damn near caused the bus going offa' the road. She lifted her skirt up. Woooh! "You see those watermelons?" I asked the guy riding two seats in front of me, the homey Racks. Had he seen Lil Momma looking like uh' Las Vegas slot machine, his eyes hit straight at attention like an over the above-satisfied spectator inside the O'Farrell's hustler's downtown San Francisco. He languished out. "I apologize havin' uh' fetish for beauty." I couldn't do anything other than respect his honesty. As I yearned to learn her perihelion, I obtained her digits while also noticing similar notions of money.

"It's hard to hold on to." Before getting back to the yards compound writing down the numbers, man! It slipped right outta my mind, what's more disturbing, can you believe ol' hatter driving the bus, gets on the loudspeaker exercising his authorities.

"Young lady driving the white Jetta, license plate number "QD101 keep pushing. You're subjected to getting pulled over for obstruction of justice." The entire bus is looking like for real homey. You jawsn, you can't be serious. Now mind you, this ol'dude looks every bit of nineteen, fresh outta' high school, just darting offa' the stage receiving his diploma. Shit, I'm only eighteen within weeks, but still old enough upon implying why he's hating on a player. Square Azz! Another inmate yells down the bus tier. "You already tricked the hook-up off, now you wanna bang on lil' momma." She didn't put up uh' fight. Who could blame that on her, as she sped off, hitting the gas. I thought, yeah, she did the right thang. Wouldn't you with dis ol' hatting azz robo? Man, I wished Adams, our other officer, was working cause right now, dang. Um, um, um! That was a touchdown scored; had I never seen one, but I'm not about to let it get the best of me. Instead, I just whipped on my hatters repellent; which, just-says- no-to bustas!

Chapter 11

ASSUMING ANYTHING IS UNHEALTHY

The Santa Rita Jail's personnel at times were often on another hype harassing us inmates over the utterly silliest rules like tucking in our shirts, don't be offa' your squares anytime we'd exited our living blocks, required us to be single-file lined up, to or from the dining room. No seconds, but the food stayed banggin' like ah' sizzler platter shrimp dish fresh off the boilers. Coolest parts, while going to the dinner, they had this one fine-ass counselor named Miss Jiffy, extra extra real thick, milk shaky like the kind outta' your favorite Baskin Robbins 31 Flavors. Fly Anita Baker timid mindset, her hips woulda' likely caused even an Ashanti to reconsider gaining uh' few pounds, her energy-four- play was quietly someplace other outta' this world. Lil momma's inner dimensions had levels that were strictly nuance. And that's keeping it casual, but if you seen her in Hollywood on Sunset Boulevard, you'd sworn highly she was ah' movie star. Her wit' was even runway material. There was just something other about her make-ups beauty, primarily undetectable to the naked eye, as she'd rang even the bells in Mars. Her IQ was proof she took life very distinctively seriously. Plenty who crossed her pathway, eyes twinkled. Even her co-workers of opposite sex, from simply just gazing, were desensitized. If hearts could speak, her smile woulda resulted in no skirtings-bail bench warrants qualifying their own penalty statutes. Just by observations, they shoulda amended the state's penal code for browsin' violations. No, for real though, she was one-of-a-kind.

She the type of person who always had the right phrases even while on purpose tryna get it wrong. Engaging dialogue with lil' momma oughta been unlawful. She was every bits official meaning of super bad, bad landmines, near hacked. I've heard stories from dudes who swear even to this day they still have permanent stains attached to their from catching simplest as a glimpse leaps of Miss Jiffy dipping through the living corridors or just thinking about her pulling up and hitting the blocks. That's on any typical day, Miss Jiffy snapped necks, which were only a portion of our daily grievances. It looked kinda as if uh' fashion show was being staged soonest Miss Jiffy's presence were known, what was forthcoming, absent though the lights and or cameras, our human acuities sockets worked like photo genetics. I myself even can pull up a shot or two from non-erasable of encounters outta my mental Rolodex, like it was just yesterday. Although our interactions were strictly unspoken, da' everlasting effects are comparable to a South Beach summer weekend Ocean's Drive Spring bling events, those delicious Hinna's, official wifey-material type, no disrespect. The perfume she played sorta had that what's-about- ism' expressively hogging on airwaves, putting icin' on her cake. Her personality couldn't get any sweeter; it'll made even sugar jealous. I almost believed one time she was kinda crushing on your boy. That's exactly why maybe assuming anything is unhealthy. I damn-neared pumped myself literally up for uh' failure just dreaming uh' bite of that. But isn't it way more guilty pleasures for denying yourself the opportunity of spar? And plus, you get nowhere not following your intuitions. "That's what's up!"

Wasn't but a handful of staff working our unit, which was not untypical, but this evening, they happened blessing our tier, letting Miss Jiffy slide working da floor. What in Heaven's land they'd open that ledge for, like ta' kicked off ah' riot. What's interesting, she couldn't have helped the situation even had she given her best efforts. Here she came floating down walkways laced in something looking every bit offa' da Prada aisle. Skin-tight powder blue-silk jean type of pants. You know how those be biting. Yeah man! They symbolized one of the famous Bay Area artist DeAndrea Drake's paintings, laminated onto a piece of the smoothest canvasses ever created, how tasteful and mouthwatering as a southern fried Lady Easter Cafe Seafoods' dish. You never visited the Bay Area durning mid Nineties, it's highly unlikely you have the slightest of sharing my pains. My God! Talking about soul food, good Lord Mighty. Had to ask myself how they'd even film the flick without offering "Miss E" uh' personal cameo or a shout-out. Wooooah! I mean, I mean! No Jawsn. But you, Miss Jiffy, um! Every step lil' momma took stated vividly. Boy, look, you bet not even think about it, cause what's over on this plate would ruin any juxtaposition in your world. But underneath my breath, I'd engaged fighting with a different conversation at the same dribbles holding my comments from escaping aloud like, "I'll rock those boots offa' your heels lil' moma', have you foaming outta da' mouth, with diamonds. But those hips, um! Had ah' bounce language that I cannot denounce, had I desired. She was politely threatening. Like, please, don't play with me! Which, if I'd veered out there what was on my mind, woulda' sent her looking for wedding dresses to this day. But it's obvious my age disqualified me then, other than it was black-eyed peas, favorite side dish, on like smothered chicken gravy and corn. They announced count time, which initiated for us inmates to be positioned at attention and, on our squares! The closer she reached my cell, my confidence was increasing for letting her get uh' piece of my mind about herself. Any time they'd given her the green light to dance through our unit, you best believe she understood my bravest thoughts, which whispered, insinuating, "Impossible was not a part of my repertoire, "believe that and too– rock on!" Holding in other discriminatory thoughts within.

"A closed mouth never gets fed" and I'm outch' here, doing my best not to glance at her ring finger. I couldn't resist, that war she won. I peeked and gotta mouth full. Her glitz woulda stopped traffic at any intersection, and her heels matched her panties, reasons I noticed the score! But that's another conversation in itself, although you know it was hard to ignore how she was making somebody other distinguishly happy, not to be questioned beyond the bounce. But, I wasn't intimidated one bit. Our eye contact was mutual and suggested wildly greatest rewards can often get discovered in keenly deep territories. You happen findin' yourself an oyster don't relinquish the bite, try ta' mount uh' knot and make the world jealous. I read exactly what she hoped she'd withstood while leaving the gates open for any unanswered questions. I'm like, that's what's up, Miss Jiffy! Thereon, my perspectives of how to love uh' women conclusively materialized from her dial.

"Hey, how you doing today, Mr. Pixar?" Man! Just why did she have ta' ask. "Better than some, worse than others, looking up and never down– now you's around Miss Jiffy." She had to double-take before responding, like... did he say what I believe, yep!

Just as sure my name's Max, and now I'm offa' my square and she's partly into her womanly feelings registering further than anything of humans pupils, despite the obligations. Further, there's exceptions not to be confused with, but I immediately caught myself, which comes almost incidental as a ghetto instinct. But it honestly was something about her mold and tastey prancing I found was a disarming force towards males in general, not only to myself. And I'm very cordial with women. Although I'm not about to get zarked out, I could give uh' damn what's on the radars. I'll not even bargain certain principals. First off, I am human- fully in tune with my sexual desires. No matter the state, there's things about us men that's non-negotiable! At least with me and my perspectives, what I believe and represent, I'll lean on. We were unduly two in-tuned adults, and I felt some kind of ways. You just gotta meet me front and center on the laminates. It was an impalpable undertone about her vibe which it hadn't sat dry. Before she was ready to leave, she asked if we could have an understanding, and I answered, scanning her bait, "It depends, probably not." In her most friendly response, she offered me her apology.

"I apologize that we aren't on similar wavelengths."

"Excuse you," I fired back instantly. "I quit school because they had too many recesses. Move how you move." She looked like, huh! What part of the game is dat? That's when I noticed I mighta hit a nerve, those kind that's humanely foreseeable, as her next response held me near naked in my imagination, not forgetting "You miss uh' hundred percent of every shot you don't take." Just saying. Those were da' last thoughts of hers which she exclaimed me to taste. when she turned departing away, I melted! Those hips on her oughta' been against the law. It wasn't much her thighs, her swag- deserved its own line of boutiques on Melrose Drive open seven days uh' week. Every part of her, from head to toe, without second thoughts. I acted iffy, as the gates begun being shut on any thoughts of any possibilities of confronting being with any other woman was dimming. I'm knowing it sounds like torture, yet I'm continuous, for it promises to be another big day. I vowed, while at the same voiced for what I believed was rightfully due upon me, which was love!

Chapter 12

OFTEN GREATEST REWARDS
FOUND KNEE DEEPEST

It's Monday morning brightly and shining. It appears the weekend ran in place, as I lost track of what I'd gotten into the entire week-ordinarily. Nature can have you leaning up against the world. Gotta stay focused and alert. Can't sleep. Anything's possible of popping off around these trenches. We're singly-filed lined up, headed for the dining room, uh' bunch of hard heads with more than enough different personalities for a lifetime. "No talking, tuck in your shirts, and no zig-zagging outta lanes. You know the routine. We do this every day, guys!!"

"Yeah, we know, it was da' same yesterday as the day before." Couldn't quite grasp who was out being outspoken, as it sparked me to look up and around over my shoulders, noticing somebody was praying for drama. This ol' geek happy-working right now. I thought to myself, "Look, do not play. Let me get outta' his way before the looks get too thick and greasy." Unable to reposition myself before singled outta' the line, damn! "Step out the line, you! Yeah Mr. Pixar," as this Mr. Robo scolded. I paused. Isn't it awfully strange how our kind always got something to say and stuck their noses into the line of fryers? But maybe that's just me over-reading the situation, who knows? I pondered.

"For what? I haven't done you much anything, Mr. Boflex," which caused his hairs to stick out.

"You know quit fronting off ah' brother in front of my superiors, don't you?"

"How's that for looking back? Boy, you Mr. Boflex, you take this job way too seriously."

"Naw, you making me do my job, pushing out there, and I'm having to answer. Got my bosses breathing down my neck, damn right! Imm do my job because you and none of these other hamburger heads gon' help me putting uh' pamper nor any bottles of milk on my tables, which nor do I intend for you to." I waged lowering the sparks, but it didn't help, as he continued.

"Listen, I have ah' new fresh born at home, you'll be out the door, I'll be without uh' gig, and the guys uh' be laughing' about how keno Mr. Boflex was. Clownin'. Look, whenever you start paying my rent, gas, and light bills, get with me. Until then, tuck your shirt in, pull up your pants, follow the rules, and we ain't got no static." As you'd say, I'ought won't no smoke. Ooooh!

The whole unit cried laughing tears, Mr. Boflex was going ham talking his Co' shit.

"Two things for certain. One thing for sure, we ain't never had no misunderstandings. It's good, Mr. Boflex." "It's obvious your interest consists of looking for better things, utilizing your daily leisure time as do plenty focused on king size hips hogging these walk-n-highways reaching way more frequencies that the law permits."

For the first time in ages, I'd given myself permission and the opportunity of having form non-judgmentals while viewing a badge. Noticing things from a different pair of eyes versus being overly selfish and quick to assume, popping off at the hip which some wouldn't likely argue deserving of another's opinion, including myself. But I cautioned while going forward, my program was on self vettings, running a tight ship, handling my bizz. Before departing, I paused upon Mr. Boflex uh' right-on- ok glare didn't say it out loud, but it eased the vibes tensions. Then I fled on about the rest of my blessed day. Into the dinner I dipped, while forcing upon myself, eating that B.S. on da' shingle. S.O.S. hard-ass-bread, cold gravy that went down like transmission fluid.

Acknowledging my past and my present as a young, respectful individual. Took recognizing the needed areas of self- discipline, which required hard self-deep evaluations. As I understood, if I ever wanted to become then or now of my fullest potential and proficient self, my own destiny had to undergo defining my character, which was difficult how it scaled upon me havin' to bachelorette. Because-okay.. yes, in reality, after applying the four levels the game prescribes, I found that it was best digesting; measuring out the rules. Granted! As they say.

"Uh' Mack is the loneliest guy in the world and must be neat and clean at any given time. He knows that any man's highly subjectively a threat upon his makings." At the same variables, I've been sorta blinded to the street life's tucked outta sight agendas in these respects, yet maintaining my differences of the status quo as a diamond in the rough, unwilling to sacrifice my principles even without fuel. I've upheld position! Regardless of the obligations, whether requiring me to re-evaluate those logistic on a regular basis in order to solidify the symbolisms as a hustler should. While doing, I've found solvency as I continue engaging forward on heart, blood, sweat, absent the fears of achieving life's goals. Whereas you might believe you've seen the best of yourself but it's going beyond limits that counts most to acquire that outer layer stepping into another set of equations. Why? Because greatest rewards often are discovered keen deepest, right?

Those are the rules to which I'm marching on as money comes without instructions, as do the different measures of life. Often at times undesigned, therefore you must be willing to freestyle with a serious love Jones to win. While alert glimpsing through life on the whims of conquering one's lucky complimentaries, which goes predominately hand-in-hand. I offer, "Heaven sent doesn't mean it's uh' fluke, cuzz what's meant to be what can dupe between." That's an excellent question.

Chapter 13

WHEN YOU HAVE A PLAN, A DISTRACTION CANNOT GROW

Monday morning it was time for court, getting prepared for pushing out in those non-heated transportation vessels. Couldn't have been viewed more distasteful. The dreadin' stood out for having to be stacked into those tight spaces for hours, caged in like animals, headed to a meat slaughter to be packed, shelved, and sold. My thoughts worked overtime on my brain nonstop. I knew it would be at least until next summer before the options of freedom was insight. Having objected repeatedly, the offers dangled three years felony probation, why, 'cause as I felt, had I pled guilty woulda' only increase the damages, making the situation more in-depth. My innocence wasn't for barter. Despite the judge was getting tired of me appearing only to reassert my rights for non-time waivers insisting motions of speedy trial. Although, I kinda knew my destination was likely prison. Yet, I reasoned to myself, What's forcing upon me to act this way? Knowing good-n-well, if I opted for a jury trial, the levels clearly were stacked against a dude, for obvious reasons. Having had no private counsel. It would likely have resulted in five years of prison terms if found guilty. That was foreseeably something to meditate upon. I'd already lost my motions for suppression on evidence. Irrespective the State withheld exculpatory evidence from our defense team. They'd wrongfully identified me. Even though they had much in my favor, the hating azz District Attorney still disagreed that a years worth of probation wasn't sufficient. Meaning law officials woulda been privy of freely searching my residence anytime they desired. I wasn't with it! Momma's crib wasn't up for those negotiations.

As I waited, pacing back and forth for the deputy sorta' to announce, You're up next, I could almost contain myself. The jailer Bailiff's keys jiggled aloud, each and every time, stomach pains resurfaced. I knew it was my number about to be dialed. "Mr. Maxwell Pixar," yells out the deputy. "What's poppin?" "You're up." "Tuck in your shirt," the bailiff instructed. "Aliiht," I answered. Mask on tight, feelings out the roof, eyes on the boards! The bailiff was kinda relaxed under the radar; it worked out for the both of us that way.

"Come out quietly with both your hands in your pockets, please. Thank you."

"Ready if you are." Just as soon as I darted the courtroom, no doubt in my mind the tripple-cross had already manifested itself. The public pretender guards flew in opposite directions even before deciding to represent my defense. As routine with majority pro-bono assistance. Although there's instances you might strike gold. But luck and me are the farthest things apart. Honestly, we've never held any such close relations.

The first words stumbled outta the attorney's mouth were ki- bosh, heart-wrenching. Serving to undermine an intended plan, freedom first, yet he opted.

"The district attorney's seeking a pretrial detention. She kinda believes your charges are qualifying and strong enough for a conviction. So, with dat in mind, the D.A.'s requesting a term of five years confinement in state prison upon if you're found guilty. The other two options, you may plead guilty today waiving your rights for a jury trial. They'd flicker but likely agree to a reduced sentence of 12 (twelve) solid months county probation, no prison term. The decision is yours for you to decide, which is a huge shifty, differs their disposition's offered before."

Now, as I'm listening to my supposedly partial mouthpiece representation of mine, offering the State's opinion, flooded theories of unsubstantiated claims, I found at best was brainwashing. I interrupted.

"Aliiht, I heard you!" But what did they promise you for serving my neck as the bait, Mr. GoodWrench?" His litty eyebrows scrunched, unsatisfied with my response as he fired back recklessly more propaganda. "That to me an insult young man." So how the fuss do you think I'm feeling with you smiling while laughing years of my precious life's at stake? It doesn't feel pleasant, now do it? "How about let's re-rock and start from square one and have a little respect for ones innocence" I projected.

His initial reactions, I gleamed he hadn't run into many with my traits, who knew and understood their rights, built for going distances. "Aye listen young man, let's not get it confused. Mr. GoodWrench prompted in his most serious, but low meaningful tone. And kept firing Lamias."

"I hope you're paying attention! It's in your very best notably to reconsider the deal they're offering you."

"How you figure that?" Stop! Wait uh' second, pump yo' breaks! These folks are talking about washing me up, sending my ass through the laundry mat fo' dry." My voice began to escalate. "Your Honor, may I approach the bench, please?"

"No, you must speak through your counsel."

Why is dat? That's what's wrong now, we cannot meet eye to eye, and our effective communications hasn't existed from the origins! And the law states that I have an absolute right to speak with my attorney in complete privacy without any third-party interferences, which consist of contact visitations in the absence of any eavesdroppings. Further, the jail's legal visitation rooms have concealed others... I've noticed a hidden video camera behind this bubble-like thing. Then I happened to glaze up, and there's a listening device attached to the rooms interior. How crazy is dat? Now I be damn! I almost yelled aloud.

"Okay, Mr. GoodWrench." The judge gestured upwards while addressing the attorneys. "Do you wish to entertain anything to what's being said pertaining to attorney client visitation rooms?"

"Well, yes, I do. Although I'm not fully prepared to present any motions at these stages, notwithstanding, we're not waiving any prejudice nor his rights upon confidentiality. But, I do believe the law clearly supports the assumptions they're not to have "any" eavesdropping capabilities in attorney-client relationships, which it's obvious they're not in compliances.

Now! I might include, the State's agents, I've asked repeatedly for a private booth to which our conversations may breathe absent any eavesdropping options into our privacy, which includes any third party's, and if I will. They've declined to adhere and, or acknowledge their own active policies of practices. But I'm optimistic with us reaching a satisfying resolution."

"Wait Mr. GoodWrench, if I might interpose on the State's behalf, Your Honor. The People were not indifferent to Mr. GoodWrench's position one way or the other. But I haven't seen any supportive case laws which say that what our agents have partaken in is a Constitutional violation. I do argue that I have no knowledge of any eavesdropping administered at the jail during legal conferences." I looked over to Mr. GoodWrench for clarification that our stated position was, in fact, not to be taken as paranoia. But no such indications followed. I knew right then I only had one solid recourse getting another counsel or representing myself. The latter I considered, being for the lack of knowledge nor funds to retain private assistance. But, yet my hood senses winked from visualizing TV shows, Law and Order, which alone it provided a suitable form of self-awareness for preparing a triable defense. I knew the basis. But that was about the stats of my observations. It's ludicrous if the state deputies were capable of intruding listing into a defendant's pretrial meetings while engaging one's attorney and investigators thereof expecting one to have any opportunities to prove innocence. "How could such be justified?" I asked myself. Like this isn't in harmony with justice, that's ridiculous! Although Mr. GoodWrench hoped to brush it off as a typical situation. Now, I'm doubting his loyalty. I insisted we needed room for us to effectively engage without any interferences, and adamantly I held to the fryer.

Given that jails are bounded branches of the States' prosecutions, it's obvious they'll notify and or alert their counter- partners about our supposedly private dialogues, whether or not it's legal, that's another question for a better discussion. Finding out the taints, it's another can of worms. Consider notions of two sports teams against each other, but one has an experienced coach, top draft picks, and elite players on their team. The other has freshmen's only. That's gotta be unrealistic illegal men down the fields. They'd squash their opponents. This ought to ring to any mindful individual being unethical, not fair play. I caught myself applyin' excuses for which wasn't making any sense. Had to ask a practical question. As I differed.

"Your Honor, if I might argue, that I would like to file a motion to relieve counsel at this time."

"Well, you cannot do that without reasonable cause." Bet'cha, I protested in contrast. Damn right! Despite the judge's cautious bites; did not stop the fuss. "What Your Honor! It's my understanding of the law if I wish, I'm able to represent myself.

Upon if I'm doing so, unforced, knowingly, willingly, and competently." In which I'm suggesting!

"STOP! Wait, wait, wait! Where did you get this information, Mr. Pixar? It appears that maybe somebody's likely given you the wrong knowledge of the law." The Judge ordered his bailiff, "Escort him out of the courtroom, please!" Whereupon we exited, leaving behind counsel and the judge for their hidden games in session, as they further exchanged.

"Okay, Mr. GoodWrench, now is the time for preliminary proceedings. Are you stipulating you're prepared to move forward?" That's not up for debate. Simple yes or no, sir? Are you, prepared?" The Judge grilled. I'm listening from the holding tank, outta sight but dialed fully in-tune, eye dribbling through a peephole adjacent the courtroom.

"I would argue to the court, I've not had a single private visitation with my client whatsoever! And I've asked the jail's captain, Mr. Paul Bloom, to acknowledge the defendant's fourth, fifth, and sixth amendment rights upon effective assistance of counsel not to be compromised. As they've yet to respond effectively for the court records, I have the signed orders. Here's my copy if you may. Mr. GoodWrench, handed the Bailiff a stack of stapled Court Orders asserting Defendant "Max Pixar's" rights for legal private attorney's confidential visitations granted, which was authorized back in July 2001 for the records."

The Judge appeared agitated in response. "Received."

"In addition to whether electronic recording devices or eavesdroppings are currently ongoing, we'll determine the basis for these effects once you're prepared to file a motion. Are you contending your defense has been breached by the jails' practices or policies for having eavesdropping into the rooms, Mr. GoodWrench?" The court drills, but counsel still was not letting up.

"Well, I didn't notice the devices until my client brought it to my attention. But based on my analysis of the law under prior holdings. It's unconstitutional for any third party to eavesdrop or have any privy opportunities of doing so "absent" notable waivers of consent as the defendant has every right to private visitations without fears of breaches or capabilities to discern privileged information. I argue that any third parties counts. For instances, police officials are highly trained experts with reading, decoding and obtaining meanings of sign languages. It's proven any of the above visuals are fully suitable for intercepting. Now, what's done with such information after it becomes obtained is beyond our control! We shouldn't be compromised for their faults."

"Well said. Has the defendant agreed upon any signed written waivers of your meetings to your knowledge?"

"No! In fact, he's fully asserted his rights, declined any legal meetings under the established practices as it sits today. We're going to trial next week, what in like seventy-two hours, and I haven't even had an opportunity to interview with my client. Over the past almost a year plus."

"Well, Mr. GoodWrench, you haven't cited any case laws which suggest your positions on the right side of justice. Nor have you noted suffered any foreseeable prejudice because of these reportedly eavesdroppings, nor am I able to find predated rulings to my understanding that'll grant you the relief you're acquiring. Therefore, we'll proceed into trial. Your motion I'll hold off until further notice."

"Your Honor," the state's attorney interjected himself into the discussions, "I'm asking a Court's Order to deny there's any such evidence of eavesdropping being unlawfully administered. And even had there been, California laws doesn't prohibit such."

"Objection, Your Honor, warrants grounds of speculations."

"Are there any offers the rooms you're being jeopardized, to which these reportedly meetings there underway? Absent consent."

"Substant," the Judge orders, leaving the States Attorney Nuva Yasuda scrambling, looking for any leads to hinge onto. Before stating coldly, "I withdraw for the record. Thank you, Your Honor!"

"Courts adjourned until noon on Tuesday, July the 27th. At such time, we'll be picking a jury, counsel. We've polled roughly 270 prospective jurors. Whether more are needed, just let us know via a motion, which is unlikely. But I'm prepared to entertain any motions for causes. Have uh' good day!" The judge slams the gavel and exits the room without further explanation.

Now I'm in distress. They've kicked me out of my own court proceedings an hour ago. I'm listening pent up against the doors peephole with my fingers crossed, in a state of tactical alert modes.

Before leaving the buildin', the bailiff approaches to ask if he could speak with me regarding my request upon recusing my attorney in exchange for self-representation.

"Mr. Pixar, let me share ah' few things with you. He who represents himself as his own counsel is considered a fool. Those realms you must know, are we clear? Just if you hadn't known." Further, they're not about to let you nor anybody else dictate how court's run, but if you're competent, you'll have every opportunity Monday morning to argue how you please for representing yourself. Just kinda throwing that out there for you to rest with over the weekend. Play if you want, without any shadows of doubt. You'll receive whatever it's your contouring."

"I'm not trophy-seeking," I inventoried.

"Glad we understood each other's prestige's for the bettering of us both." Yet, I paused! Noting he's covered first-hand the results of other defendants who'd placed before asserting their options for self defenses at their own quest mittens. The keys of ways gathered were put on a seatbelt, don't be caught loose!

But I wasn't about to show any signs of aversions. I vowed, "It is what it is." Further, when you have a plan, a distraction cannot grow. I hadn't slightest inferences of losing, therefore the only angel of which was on my agenda, stay focused!

"Well, Mr. Aswad, the judge's not about to go back-n-forth with you, so make up your mind, hold in thought right whereas you at." I'm looking outta orbits, Lost in space like, "Negro-have- you-lost-your-damn-mind!! You better take that damn probation and be outta here on the next thing smoking." Or keep on!!!

The bailiff caught my attention just as I begun sweeping the floor with my eyelids.

"Listen, young man, do yourself a favor, and don't speak during court unless you're spoken upon to. That'll save yourself some heartaches down the road."

Chapter 14

THE OL' ELEPHANT DANCING IN THE ROOM

While some think it would be game over up against a created design when you're forced to defend yourself suppressed to or compelled from engaging counsel under restraints. But I hadn't given up faith in our Constitution, which reads unfeatherly, without room to suggest indifferently. "Every person charged with a crime has an absolute right to engage with counsel in privacy free from third parties whose preferences are subjectable under opposite notions." Importantly, I declined the non- waivers, free of self harms. Why should a person surrender one right to assert another? This hadn't made any sense, given the amendments provide full protection rights upon conversing with one's counsel, "privately." Which oughta include absent being subjected to fears of third parties who may obtain sensitive private subjects helpful to another person's defense. I argue having any law officials or agents capable of deciphering supposedly privileged convos unduly, inappropriately is beyond outta bounds. Thus, whether videotape usage or human persons are the exact terms of the extensions of eavesdropping and identical in context. Although I'm not an attorney, it's common knowledge and doesn't require a rocket scientist to understand "us" humans with the very simplest forms of everyday life skills can determine a person's mood, feelings, inferences, position of substance, and so forth, from gazing through any continual steady position whether utilizing a human or the naked eye! The results are the same tainted on their basis of its origin of ordinances.

Even a baby reads humans' body language, hand motions, and facial features, not to underscore those with an honor badge they're trained to detect the virtues of one's intentions who's placed under watchful measures, which means their fully receptive of a person's conversation in debits, absent audio listing post. Visual observations in itself speak loads of volumes! It's not only humans who have those basic instincts. But since we're speaking of the human aspects, let's not lose focus. Internal visions of a ferocious breach of ultimate due process rights upon to engage with any legal defense party while preparing for jury trial is unreasonable without first having at least one nondistracted conversation with an attorney, absent his or her waivers of consent, which requires the jailer/sheriff of each county for upholding the justice due process doctrines. Enforcing a means of open two-way dialogues with a person's attorney before and or during trial holds universal cause preventing mischievous deeds. It's disastrous to think otherwise for insisting any person held to answer any proceeding, whether guilty equal protections, it's unmarginalized to think otherwise. Says the forefathers of our bedrock Constitution requires reasonable safeguards!

The rights upon presenting compelling evidence to assist engaging one's own defense, and the rights non abrogated with attorney's unfeathered assistances. "Right or wrong?" I'm just stunned with any litigations if forced upon opposite, the legal advice under instances as those out stated oughta therefore be viewed such as recreational, can't be taken seriously.

For starters, consider an atmosphere that's infected within within living units, housing quarters, in which interviewing rooms for legal conferences are placed under opened corridors, and any person within distances has the ability to observe and eavesdrop without a person's permission or knowledge. That's weird! You're in an 8' by 10' room, and counsel is positioned opposite the divider. You know how a regular jail cell room looks. Only these have dividers between you, induced with a speaker microphone amplifying device, transferring your voices from origin through reception, tweaked full volume, enabling the whole unit to listen and overly discern what's regarded as privileged information, coupled with video recording devices feeding into the deputy's booths. Whether it's also synonymous and, or debatable, humans, we're recorders, hold information obtained otherwise stored into our held thoughts. It's laughable to begin arguing in protest differently. One cannot hold a straight facial feature looking at me to suggest another perception. A deputy who's monitoring a person placed under these restraints over any such extended time frames, let's say a month of weekly observations, approximately an hour per visit, wouldn't they be of attendance of the substance or directions of the actual parties' inferences or intended basis of their dialogues. "That's only the tip of that iceberg." Now spread those cavities of monitoring over twelve- fourteen consecutive months. The results, imagine walking on eggshells. The damages life changing upon the aggrieved parties. It's not unfantasy. There is no inference under the sun. I could oppose other than over worked, underpaid attorney's dubious mind frames, which have the nerve of thoughts. One's defense isn't invaded or trampled on.

Maybe sufficient to his or her own appetite to isolate a person's position for the other party's agenda. Maybe am I insinuating at those symptoms of such hindrances violate the nexus of our United States Constitutional foundation under any pretenses and should ring throughout the whole West Coast's judicial branches. It's no submerging. How's any Presiding Justice able to permit and or ignore the strikes at the hearts upon justice which now the beacons upon shined? It's hard maintaining a straight posture and insist within good morals of standards how they wouldn't gain the highest conviction numerals throughout California.

There's one particular incident in which a dude alerted me of an insecurity. He stated they hadn't had knowledge of a certain piece of evidence on his case, but as soon he went and interviewed with investigators and his counsel, the officials went out to the scene of his crime and retrieved the tainted evidence. Like before, drawing the distinctions of notions of two teams gambling, although one has the upper hand of from knowledge. Could you imagine a situation of a person who's up against decoys positioned in the opponent's huddles of practices prior to a game day to discover full tentative of players routes, hard counts for hikes. It would be devastating beyond landslides on the adversaries. Not only does it increases chances of winning, it's unfathomable to unnotice the despair that's fancy scared.

Look, there's players who's not done a tenth of what I'm implying as simplest as mishandling, the tool the "games rock." You've seen how they ridiculed guys before, repeatedly in and outta court on restitution—almost ruined one guys' career. Yeah, there's rules, which are set out at the beginning of each formal game. "Life's no different." For which functions as a persons baseline of guidance on fairness. Notice the foundationals, whether intentional or mistake and or it's notable excusable neglects. You'll have to abide to its held practice and penalties. "Illegal man down the field." ruffing the quarterback after whistle's are blown. Those kind of flagrant you have to rely on and anticipate what's next, as I would suppose justice ought not, therefore, to be excluded or too far behind.

I'm askin' candidly where's our hoods' referees when we're unjustly fouled, hit below the belts, rejected outta the game for objecting to avoid resulting holding court in the streets! Who out there rejoicing in having whistles disbursed throughout our city ghettos? But something has to give otherwise; it's kinda Hummer Square how we're living and being treated. Stay mindful, as if I'm speaking a foreign language. Just as if chronic pains at times require an orthopedic evaluation, they aren't able to withstand. Kinda hard to expect any person to ignore being placed under extensive restraints and third parties' breaches of privileged reasonable expectations of privacy zone, which extends to a person's home, cars, places where you're engaged with private actions. Containing one's innocence is best notated in the Hallmarks of favorite, our "Miranda Rights." Thus, I believe starts the very second you're placed under arrest. And if you're fighting back defending, do you lose those rights?

The right of retaining your silence, against any self-incriminations. Because anything you say can and likely will be used against you in a court of law. But now it appears extended to personal opinions, or have I miss or forget something. People are being tried in the public's perceptions for opposin' against the rights that are supposedly free, the right to breathe freely and choose your pathways of life, which comes in different forms. But privacy doesn't relinquish itself! What if you discovered your shirt popped open while you're speaking to the opposite sex? I know that's uh' stretch. But shit happens. Even those actions consist of obtaining rebounds. Just saying thinking outside the box; travels distances with a variety set of principles. But is it sufficient to invade the other person's private space "absent" initial consent or causes? Fact of tha matter inducing electronic devices into a person's privacy without waivers is full fledge comedy deserving its own prime spot on "Netflix." The very symptoms of these held circumstances violates the nexuses of everything we consider fare play upon any pretenses. Imagine dat! Yeah, I'm from East Oakland, where our youngsters getting modest; blow it!

"Your Honor, may I approach the court with a motion?" I argued repeatedly in self-defense.

"No, you have to speak through your counsel." As the judge often admonished in his bias attitude to assert, mind you!" Do not forget who's running the show. But I couldn't let it slide and voiced, "I've alerted the attorney, Your Honor, numerous times, but to which no satisfying responses were followed." As I maintained my non-negotiable principles declining to become substituted to avoiding my gut wrenching feelings. Yet forced to act out my age, as ghetto terms mandated once placed into a danger zone, we fight with whatever tools at our disposable. "Right?" Not quittin, nor letting our foot off the gas.

"Your Honor, there's rules to which our Constitution provides a defendant who's asserting his right for counsel, in part requires that Justice be equal to the oppositions while defending his or her rights. Upon, as I erupted during open court, raising more than just eyebrows of counsel, the judge and States' prosecutor—couldn't ignore what was fetched. "Like I said, Mr. Pixar, you have no position of speaking without unless through your counsel." The judge continuously denounced my multiple requests, leaving me questioning Mr. GoodWrench counsel to defend, but only to be slanted from voicing what was obvious, "The ol'elephant dancing in the room." Imagine a circus full of magicians. Although, the partial mouthpiece for hire provided at state expenses, he did have on his most expensive suit, no Jawsn.

Yet still to be discerned! The judges only commits were "Okay, thank you next." Despite the attorney's arguments that our conferences were exposable, he still failed to offer any meaningful resolutions to which we were able to openly communicate. You knew without saying there was an unusual mischievous dial. Thus, even on mute, it created discomfort. The judge adjusted his eyewear, and the only thing heard or seen was his black robe hugging da' corners of the bench, slapping his gavel while simultaneously uttering, "Court's adjourned!" I'm like, ouch! That looked like it hurt, yet as he disappeared, the sounds like a Nascar driver consumed on, zooooom! His glasses positioned near slipping offa those nostrils. I looked towards counsel praying he'd seen the same. We held equal glares out at each other like barbeque or mildew. You know those stories rarely end with happy endings. Before counsel had an opportunity to speak, bailiffs were pulling on my trousers.

"We're done. Keep moving, Mr. Pixar." Quite usual, what was about to follow next. We vanished out through the rear of the building's courtroom, which is primarily reserved for defendants going up state.

And there you found me posted cocky fully shackled head to toe, ankles included biting tighter than uh' virgin's vice grips, Boy! If that wasn't uh' monkey wrench, where was I, flying uh' kite, never preparing for a safe landing? Imagine dat!

Chapter 15

OFF THE DRIBBLE

Your Honor, before the jurors are sworn in, the defense wish filing some proposed requests under the voir dire's questionnaires in specific, we'll be raising the first request that any seated juror whom may have had a close friend and or family that was ever charged or arrested of a crime whether civil or criminal it be revealed to the defense for of possible prejudices or biases.

The court acknowledges– upon proceedings from counsel Mr. GoodWrench's request.

"Motion granted to the defense request next motion the judge began to move our proceeding rapidly, the standards, voir dier motions takes its courses of actions before the trial starts, which is designed to give each side the opportunity to raise arguments that which might possibly result into somewhatz level playing field. But you know it's undoubtedly not gonna' be equal justice until the laws are amended. But it's a process where state prosecutors presenting its case who may of instance, be pursuing for the rights of impeaching and or introducing other fatal evidence to make the defendant appear they're this horrible person, referred to as "Moral Turpitude Evidence." They'll seek to utilize that for degrading a person's character. Whether it's the victim and or the defendant that's on trial, isn't it supposed to work both ways. But often, prosecutors withhold and hide favorable evidence from the defense only to give their teammates better positioning for plea bargaining. It's a surreptitious invasion up against those who'll fight back, which, in my view, appears clearly forms of obstruction of justice. While attorneys tend to know of such tactics but seldom prepare ahead, letting the opposition off the hook.

And my next request, "Objection, Your Honor."

The state's attorney, in her most fervent and yet passionate voice, interrupted.

"The People wishes to introduce its first request before the defense proceeds, please."

"Okay—thank you, your motion's granted. If you would please state your position." Upon the Judge acknowledged the state's request.

"Thank you, Your Honor! The state's attorney began arguing their avalanche of B.S. A motion to exclude any arrest suffered from one of its key victims on unlawful misconduct from a January 2002'ish incident outta San Francisco, California, an hour's distance from Oakland. They'd tapered opposing whether its victims were involved with running an unlicensed gambling shack from their home as a place of business in which upon believed it was staged from the start.

"The defense holds evidence the state's engaged with an act of colorful intimidations, falsely arresting one of the victims weeks before the trial in order to bargain, pressure and proposition her to assist the state, which in my contentions were forms of another obstruction of justice. Couldn't a soul distract me to believe otherwise."

"Your Honor, both of these offenses were dismissed at the States' urgings." The prosecutor offers.

"Are the defense seeking to question "Miss Malibu" for the defendants opposing arguments, Mr. GoodWrench?"

"Yes, I do believe gambling is a crime of moral turpitude, and I would, if she denied there weren't any type of such activities going on at the establishment, and I believe this unquestionably would be grounds for impeachment of her," Mr. GoodWrench bluffs.

"Ms. Yasuda for the people, Your Honor. May I respond to those arguments?"

The judge agrees, "Yes. But I'll give you my tentative thoughts if you may haven't noticed at preliminary proceedings Miss. Malibu denied that she or any other person had ever engaged in gambling there on their property, and there just might be a good faith basis to bring the request like what's implied of in light of this January's arrest, Ms. Yosuda."

"That's well put, I would agree, Your Honor. Had there been any evidence about the basis of this arrest, and it happened within San Francisco county lines. There are not any police reports of this incident. Nor do I know whether or not she was charged and held to answer. But our held position is it hadn't risen to the level of criminal violations. It says no report was filed and no evidence the victim here's involved." The Court interposes with a position in order to fashion its permutations.

"We could assume, based on the evidence, simply had there were any tables and or unlawful gambling—dice, cards, and other forms of equipment utilized for sole purposes of gambling, cheat sheets, and those types of things. But right now as I do not have the authority to examine the actual evidence that hasn't been presented. But if charges were ultimately filed then later dismissed, there had to have been a police report numbered somewhere."

The judge was adamantly concerned without stepping over the lines as the intensity drew and grew a mustache.

"Well, I would respectfully disagree, Your Honor. Had there existed any type of evidence surrounding this arrest and it happened within the San Francisco district, I do not let me say the charges were missed. And I'm unaware of the reasons. The judge asks: "Now my question for the defense is, "Have you made any efforts to get these reports, Mr. GoodWrench?"

"Me, no."

"And how have we learnt this today, Ms. Yasuda?"

"I notified the defense, but I am not conceding it amounts to a contact of moral turpitude as I disagree that it's admissible." The judge stated his preset position scattered.

"Okay, in the court's view, I do not see any cases whether or not of gambling is a crime of moral turpitude. But it's likely she'll disagree she was ever as much involved, but you have no police reports for disputing her for impeachment purposes. Counsel for the defense, you should had further investigated this. That's your fault. However, erroring on the facts. You may ask her good faith questions whether or not she was ever of involved with gambling, approaching or inducing an officer to engage with gambling, that sorta' thing. But the questions have to stop there without any supportive evidence such as Police reports, photos, and, or the arresting officer available to introduce the unlawfulness acts."

Defense counsel, your needed inputs we'll do following voir dire. The next round of motions oughta' settle any questions for which pertain to Ms. Malibu."

"Thank you, Your Honor. Our defense next motions are the exclusions of evidence on any moral turpitude or other arrest, and I would include that Mr. GoodWrench's motion includes or seek bifurcations which prohibit any references to the defendant Mr. Pixar's "Parolee status" fully!"

Thus, the State cannot alert the jury directly and nor indirectly of Mr. Pixar's arrest about his prison served time before, and let's be sure to put uh' sign up somewhere. The jurors are not to learn of the nature of Mr. Pixar's parolee status and or anything to do with him being charged with any crimes as the defense has argued it's instrumental with sensitive fundamentals towards their defense, any terms relating to the such language of "Parolee at large" in or directly, are supposedly be excluded from the jurors unless it's otherwise ordered by a motion first, and outside the juror's presence, both parties. Are these orders clear?"

"Yes, Your Honor." Both attorneys, in unison, stipulated.

"Be sure to admonish your agents and any persons you may be considering on your intended list for arguments of positions. And the final motion the defense has asked there be at least one juror of those seated they be of his racial ethnicity, gender nor race doesn't matter." Noticing myself, courts have routinely found there's a rule of law, whereas if there's a distinctive group involved identifiable with immutable characteristics. Such exist and cannot purposefully be excluded. A distinctive group is found such as African and Mexican-Americans are distinctive groups, Asians, Hispanics, and Indians likewise are distinctive, women, and men. The law forbids racial discrimination in the selection of jurors and only requires the juror's venire process to extend upon which jurors are petted representing a fair cross-section of one's community.

Of starters, if they are on the Venire list, the actual panel of persons, which makes up twelve jurors upon to be petit and seated. It's my position that they'll summon a party with a diverse panel to choose from, but as soon they start picking of those to be seated, the blacks outta nowhere profoundly disappears. Meaning they'll not even get the opportunity to be petited for of seatings. They'll have the list of 260 potential jurors, and in some cities, it'll be possibly maybe 10 blacks outta the 12 jurors, and not one will have the opportunity to be even possibly considered. Almost more times than not, they're discriminated against and voided out at the early stages.

Why? It's a virtue they'll make certain any jurors whom's reportly your peers are positioned at the bottom and never have the time of day to get even outta their seats for the questioners. That's where examinations of any biases commence—providing interest on life's measures. It's widely believed you must first establish a prima facie violation of jury unfair examinations. Whereas a defendant must present bias evidence in order to overcome those barriers. By proving the group excluded was a "distinctive" class of one's community. Well, in my proposition, if you've never given me the options, that in itself outta' rise to a natural form of inherit bias. Not a single black petited for the test. It's beyond playing with a person's intellect in a game of three- card molly. You know how they'll have three tops, and one appears to have something underneath, and the shuffle begins? You'd swear you seen it, but soon as you indent yourself saying, I found it. Abracadabra, now you see it, now you don't! That's how the jurors get fadangled while petited, which it's a silent form of hidden measures of bias. But they'll never disclose the brilliance of shade, yet it fortunately does exist. And depending on your make-up, maybe- certainly has the whereby pitch for an appeal, but there are thousands whose lives were stolen right underneath these very hidden agendas.

What I've learned about the human race of any ethnicity, we are known to make unusual sets of split decisions. When we get together as one grow like voting, it's not a myth. Ponder upon if only one distinctive group were permitted to vote on the outcome of any debate, not excluding the general elections, wouldn't it be predictable? Which is one of the oldest forms of suppression of a vote. How would you not notice these same principles of practices that expands to permit any ethnicity to vote. As including women. Shouldn't it apply to jury trials against unequal protections of the "voir dires" processing? Not to underscore the equal right of a balanced seated jury. No one distinctive group or class ought ta preside over a person's fate containing no shared qualities. Defined as the rules of law, the best for distinctiveness is whether a person invested holds qualities that define him or her as a group. Such individuals may exhibit similar beliefs, experiences, and attitudes not to ignore what racial group they're from. Whether White, Asian, Hispanic, Black, or Indian– those are of distinctive characteristics and must be applied correctly in any determinations upon any debatable selections. And even still, if no one's reportedly paying attention how votes possibly can appear then disappear. Thank God for vast presence at those formulas of work– otherwise, who knows how our world would look right now? Numbers don't lie, nor does inherit bias while you may wish inept what I'm feeling isn't happening. But I promise you if you place any distinctive group to sit through a trial of twelve opposite characteristics and if they're elderly don't try even thinking about it! It's nearly unanimous that the results to follow, whether guilty or innocent, would never hold a level playing field. Simply put, and that's any racial component, distinctive group with identifying traits.

Notice the word itself distinctiveness; it speaks for itself. Racial jury exclusion discrimination has gone on for too long of our lifetimes. It's unjustified for any ethnicity to have to be tried with any jury that's not his or her peers. Meaning at least "one" juror that shares what our Constitution zeals, the Sixth Amendment, in fact, forbids those forms of discrimination in the selection of jurors and requires the venire from which jurors are petit be a diversely selected representation of a fair-various, of its sector from one's community. It helps to avoid pressure and any influences on outcomes to be sought, acting sorta as an equalization.

Some argue, and I must respectfully disagree, that a petited jury itself need not represent a fair cross-section. Yet it's been proven more so than not one's ability to show there's inherent intentions for excluding a distinctive group of the community. Again, if they've never placed into a determination of the factors, that in itself holds an exclusion with intent. Although hidden– often as they'll initiate to induce unlawful electronic devices, it's the nook, that ol' elephant dancing in the room. It's only because no referee has yet sounded the alarm on the foundational infrastructures nor our elected officials of such process-prohibiting of the then-numbered seated jurors must be diverse and simi- balanced to at least give an identifiable distinctive group with immutable traits their fair chances at Justice. Whether it be race or gender surrounding these ethnicities, the options for even to have become tested for the seat of one of the twelve (12) jurors' position, it's clearly foul play when you have a defendant on trial and not a sole person looks like him or her, nor share anything in common. A total of twelve opposite "disparities" to the defendant whose da' gripe about, and that's only the gulf of the surface of unequal treatments. Its fundamentals are enticingly unfair, one of the primary reasons our urban streets are packed with marchers. In my opinion, criminal branches of the quazy judicial structures are unjust sleepily parked, appearing to have blindfolded the obvious facts. Let's not exclude those unforgotten who mighta never had an initial fair opportunity and given life sentences.

You have "FBI" agents blowing their own inner whistles on racial injustices. None of their own kind are being promoted into higher positions of power. Yeah, they're on the squad part of the force but not seated at the tables where decisions are being determined. That's fact, not fiction, and its of possible had there wasn't ordered certain mandates at certain giant Google tech institutions for some forms of diversity, Lord knows where we were likely headed. They're getting better, and as our world evolves, we as Americans, have to extend our better ways by uniting our U.S. citizens. We owe ourselves a form of humility to our due process agenda also. And yes, "words do matter." That's the reason individuals deserve to be re-evaluated considerably with a level playing field where there appears situations with any of opposite distinctive group excluded from his or her traits, including Jury procedures outta be given an opportunity to be re-evaluated with a level playing field, with at least one of his or her own racial ethnicity group. Or to be relinquished of liabilities. That's the very least we as a society can expect, and hope a mandate's forthcoming from our lawmakers and or judicial branches of power. But to keep on the same path as there's nothing wrong, I'm just not comprehending any similar feelings–those fannings. The right to defend one's position fairly without biases, untainted nine times outta ten would solve portions of our united American grievances. It, of course, has to be retroactive as this in absence leaves our initial retribution clauses unresolved "because what's good for the goose has to be good for the geese"–right or wrong? But it's only if lawmakers are serious and or honestly interested in what's facing our nation, for fully rebounding on the right footings. But they're hiding the real consensus if something is to ever change within our society today, it's gotta' be seen as a genuine reform with widespread reconciliations every human person worldwide, not some but the whole! Holding a bipartisan stimulation for our nation moving forward as redefined. Enlisting equal treatment for every human person worldwide and it's gotta' start from the top with a mandated order, or anything otherwise, it'll be received as mischief with no stimulus capabilities moving our nation towards of rightful projections as leaders of the free world. Examine how our world of sportsmen and or women, participation with social issues motivates and uplifts the voices and values of our society, letting their talents act as vehicles for those of the unforgotten while bringing visuals to the forefront; otherwise it wouldn't amount nearly half the things which exist today had there existed only one ethnicity group. Those are simple examples of unity works in margin approaches. Not having particular prones of instance. You have Whites, Asians, Hispanics, and Blacks playing in the world of sports, muddy puddles, and they'll hug afterward despite if they've won or lost. Nice game, bruh! That's how our world is supposed to filter. It shows our youth coming behind. These are the fundamentals of fairness. Thus, how can any justice sit idle, unmoved presiding with not a single Black juror deciding any black defendant's fate by twelve opposite?

It's gotta be unfathomable to watch without feeling some kind of way, and that's just "Off The Dribble!"

Chapter 16

THESE THOUGHTS OF MINES

We are back on the record for the defendant Maxwell Aswad Pixar who is present with counsel. Miss Yasuda here for the People. We'll bring in the jury. I'll read out the instructions, and then we'll discuss opening arguments." As I quivered, the judge began infusing his orders for the jury trial, which was upon underway.

"Mr. GoodWrench, my clerk says you and your counsel boths inquired about hardship forms. We'll get to those right before the jurors are seated."

"Your Honor, if I might please advise the State of our other very important lengthy pretrial conferences, not to mention or make any references to my client in custody status and, or his "parolee conditions. Agreed such actions by the State would invoke biases that's an unerasable and incite jurors with measures of taint beyond inspirable."

"Thank you, Mr. GoodWrench, for kindly alerting us again today to your concerns, as the people were previously given earnest, timely notices on how to avoid breaching Mr. Pixar's due process rights!

It's listed throughout your motion papers and our discussions yesterday, and I hope they'll keep an eye out on the direct orders and instructions of mine." I'm posted listing it's beyond puzzling searching Mr. GoodWrench for his reactions which maybe slipped over my head. As if anything he's asked of wasn't my Constitutional right. But okay! I'm kinda discombobulated by how the Judge pushes him to the side bar. I'm like, you stay alert Mr. GoodWrench. I'm doing the exact same, as I found zero sense of freedom looking to make eye contact with counsel who stared inopposite which appeared to have scaled any unsaid fearfulness. As you're just another docket for of judicial process. But too implied, not so quickly, you're worthy more than just a number. Although, I might not have had fully understood his arguments. But I'd given him the benefit of the doubt. This was new ta' me, jury trials. I've only watched snippets on live TV and still hadn't quit gotten the full sweeping meanings. But if it applies, I'll be perceptive and mindful. The court began instructing the jurors and explained. There's a presumption of innocence, and the State has the burden of proof, which lies for the prosecution of proving, since the defendants pleaded not guilty. Do not look, nor let outside biases distract your thoughts. We'll learn how far that holds for proving beyond any reasonable gripes and leaving the room for open interpretations! Entirely-that was a hard conversation with myself. What exactly had that mean! It's was much too late for biting the nails, nervous monotones, gotta be precise, or I'm doomed! But I'm receptive that's never gonna happen.

The Court spoke again. Almost impossible to determine the gravity of its intent, but O'well, here we go!

"Alright. Let us proceed. We're ready with Mr. Pixar now, who's presently assisted by counsel. Mr. GoodWrench and the People, by the States attorney Miss Yasuda, also present." May we. Real quickly, Your Honor. "Never mind. It's ok!"

Fast forward two days. Trials roughly halfway through, and I'm almost about to grab counsel mid-sentence. The detectives just received an admonishment not to make any references to my parolee status. Maybe, though, that's not what I believe to have overheard. Sounded awfully close. Further, the states reported victim only speaks that Italian foreign language, which I'm not gettin' how he's working at our local ghetto neighborhood storefronts, and now he's begun feigning incapabilities of interacting effectively with the English language. But I'm not about to speak for him. He's got a language interpreter, which is good enough. Anyhow, he's the attorney. I'll let him handle what its he retained and paid for. That's his, not my, lane. They're reaching overboard though with frivolous questioning. They're now saying I punched him and ran outta the store with ah' six-pack of beer; lying through their teeth, what I wasn't suppose to object! That's what my hired attorney's supposedly for, or am I? Hell, I wouldn't know. Nor am I in a position to debate with my life on the edge. And the obvious, it appears nothing other than a stakeout. Twelve opposite opinionated jurors, which says what? Guilty before the verdict forms were thought up or ever being created. Light but wry. I asked the opted counsel how are they to have twelve white jurors, and I'm a young Black youth. Aren't those unfair laterals? You know their response? They are only required to give you a group of twelve that's your peers, "my peers." Yeah, that's where we lost connection.

As I know he's got on glasses, as does the judge and States prosecutor. But it doesn't undermine what my Constitutional guarantees are supposed to be—the right of equal protection under the law. I hadn't waived any rights for a jury reflective of my peers.

Now I be damn! I'm outta my district for a crime which, in essence, had nothing to do with me. They've utilized this ol' store event to put me under arrest, enabling the search of my vehicle. That's how the weapon came about the loaded Glock handgun. So they say it was placed hidden atop of the wheel of my tire. That's garbage. Get the hell out of my way. I fought the hardest to keep my thoughts to myself and in check from slippin' outta my trap. But the unclaimed was worth me voicing my opinion. Then again, maybe not.

Chapter 17

PRESUMPTIONS

Detective Nickles, how did Mr. Pixar become a targeted lead suspect during his initial encounter with San Francisco P.D. Officers? Were you guys requested there to the store or happened to just be near the area and stopped and noticed some commotions?

"Well, our initial intent was that one of our field officers noticed the defendant's vehicle was descriptively wanted for another incident, and the surveillance was then directed to his attention. It was soon thereof provided via media news channels alerting a significant danger for the public, and I hadn't wanted staling getting that out there. We've got uh' "felon at large" who's possibly armed and may be dangerous. I felt there was an urgency with releasing this out into media outlets."

"Wait-wait-wait! Objection, Your Honor. Mr. GoodWrench stormed in outrage for the States detective alerting the jurors regarding Max's parolee status, the very evidence the judge ordered and prohibited not to let become exposed. They superseded their boundaries for not protecting of the defendant's rights, "presumption of innocence." I almost sprang from outta my seat. But I knew better that woulda given the states bailiffs ah' free pass for disarming their weapons. It's kinda happened several times before-where supposedly the officer felt threatened and, out of safety concerns, feared and opted to discharge their service weapons upon innocent lives. Although I'm not suggesting a person doesn't have the right to defend against oppositions whether not they're officials or not, that's our given American right. But opening my parolee status for the juror's speculations wasn't for the debates as it shouldn't have never gotten revealed. It was ruled predetermined. But still, you know I knew better. That woulda' given the Bailiff's uh' free pass. Just sayin'! How's now? We're supposed to expect there's not any non-preconceptions? The Judge couldn't help but to intervene as the twelve jurors exited the room with casual stares, but unfriendly, to say the least.

"Let's approach the bench counsel, may we?" Whereas upon Mr. GoodWrench was a nervous wreck. Why, I'ought' know how. They're the ones whom violated the rules, not us. Ain't it ironic how when you're not even the one who's in the wrong but yet you're spooked? That's how crazy it's become, which appears designed to sink the defendants' confidence if you're at opposite ends of the justice bar. It just goes with da territory. Catch your breath now, Max. I verbatim to myself, hold tight do not lose your vibe.

The court opinioned, "Mr. GoodWrench, I'm certain you like to have an opportunity of being now heard on the facts whether or not the State has compromised your clients' rights and in violation of my pretrial orders involving Mr. Pixar's rights having his parolee status excluded and kept outta the jurors conversations. Have I correctly described your issues?"

"Well, yes, Your Honor." That's absolutely my position. And, I would be seeking a motion for another jury to be promptly impaneled, being you've admonished the State repeatedly not to disclose any content of the defendant's parolee status. We've filed proper motions way ahead of time to avoid these very bridges of abrogations. They'll say it wasn't intentional, nor was any harm done. But still, they've breached of barriers, shifting the pace of defendant's chances of any impartialities. Was it purposeful? Holds for a multiple choice.

Regardless, we're insisting on a different panel of jurors. There isn't any such thing as unringing the bell. It cannot! Which in the best interest of justice, there's not any means to rewind the effects of bias if attached to the defendant and must not, therefore, be viewed unrungable. That taxi departed the station. Its destination, we don't or won't know. Let's not waste unneeded time on vetting what these jurors are contending. I would ask there be a rulin' in favor for the defense in the best interest of justice—a mistrial.

"Well, Mr. GoodWrench, I would agree, but I'm interested in what Miss Yasuda has to offer for the People's position. If she'd weigh in, please. Which, I'm sure you hadn't intended for that to be lead out there, but it's done which shouldn't be sidestepped nor misplaced." Now I'm looking baffled almost lost for words waiting yet, only sketching the damages before the Court revered further. "His parolee at large status went far beyond opening up cans of worms. But I would like to believe that my instructions to the jury to ignore what was wrongfully exposed was cured, but it was quite a significant violation Miss Yasuda."

"Yes, Your Honor, you've stated well, I hadn't intended for that to spill out into jurors' conversations. But, I forgot to take the time to admonish my agents that were on my debunks. I do apologize." Thinking how gaped-minded. That rebooked the rest of my afternoon. That's where we collided. I lashed out. "You say what! I fought to reinforce. Listen, Miss women, my life's at stake on the table you finna' leave soonest courts adjourned.

You're headed home to your family. I have to recede with a smile for your mistakes of error, as a no intended cause of action. That's jawsn, and you know it! "Mr. Pixar, you're not to interrupt my courtroom. I'm running this in here. Now, if you do not follow these orders, you'll be politely escorted out."

"That's bullshit, Your Honor! Where were you when my precious rights were being trampled upon and taken advantage of? Who was interested in my freedom of due process, and they've done these things with a purposeful intent for obtaining a one- sided outcome." Although instructed not to induce any taints, they've acted outta deception to tarnish my reputation. Now they're expecting the courts leniency, for another look to dissuade the same twelve jurors they've not heard, "being of an ex-felon," which violates more rights than one, as I thought to myself. Did you notice how those thirsty eyes looked with smirks, dashing across their facial features dishearteningly, insinuating. Yeah, I'm checking! Do not even think about getting off without putting up your A-games fight. I'm like, damn! Wooa, are you serious?" The judge suddenly upon imposed his orders, instructing the bailiff to "take him to the holding tanks." As we began in motion, I initiated the fight of my life, resisting everything but time served. While it was obvious their agendas towards handling adversities from a single-lens perspective became null, which only further acknowledges ethics, and of society's growth which looked parasailing the wrong direction. As I'm being escorted off the dance floor, I'm being scuffled up roughly, but it hadn't stopped proceedings of the subject matter. The judge whisked on. "Miss Yasuda, I am not in the least bits faulting you that you hadn't admonished the detective, as I believe you were caught off guard between giving your questions and receiving of the answers. Maybe it was a mistake. However, it had the depths exposing his ex-felon status. But, in my view, the court's admonishment to the jury was broad enough to satisfy any biases the jurors may have had. I'm going to perceive at first glance, and at heart, you did not intend for it to slip out as it shouldn't have happened. But I immediately was responsive to any likelihood of taints, and I'm finding no prejudice, although how unfortunate of the fact."

Chapter 18

AFTERHOURZ

Having discovered the needed strength and power to get through these rough days, which hadn't always come without their ups and downs. Yet, I found the guts looking through an undistorted mirror. I understood perfectly what it cost to defend an assertive position, whether innocent or guilty. Realizing in spite justice is better served where your coins match your heart. Not that I'm undermining State's pro-bono mouthpieces. There are results without retainers. But your chances are slim to none, while noticing paying for counsel doesn't outright guarantee freedom. But the rules somewhat differs as opposed to hired help. No questions, you snap open that wallet. Shit tends to happen quicker than lightening speed. That's nothing unlearned, only for further acknowledgements. Keep receipts for the gouch, bet! I hoped to avoid choking an eagle offa' the back of uh' nickel. Indeed upon standing your ground has its fundamentals. Thinking quickly, not slick, knowing your next move gotta' be your best, and visualizing steps ahead is often rewarding. But on this journey, I'm unashamed to announce that it's those nautilus. Gotta be uh' sailor ahead, meaning getting "money without being penalized." It's forever the brow.

The week has been shocking, a real bummer! Convicted on majority of the charges, at least the serious ones. Possession of a controlled substance and the weapon counts. Although, they dismissed the driving on suspended licenses and petty store violations, which, compared with my other two felonies, was cookies-n-gleam. The ol' district attorney, boy, did he argue tooth and nail for a maximum term of five years to run consecutively, as I hoped for the latter bowlegged terms, meaning serving time for one crime while getting credited for the others. Now, as the judge continued reading aloud the harsh sentence; I'm finding it more and more difficult to listen, looking behind tryin' to gather who in the hell might they be referring to. Damn, surest wasn't me. But they stated without doubt, "Mr. Maxwell Pixar" as I answered hesitantly, dipping out there with my two-cented jabs in defense of proposed rights invaded.

The guards and everybody fought with tryna lower the brows while calming me down, which didn't help the growl. The Judge displayed his most threatening tone and continued on. "Mr. GoodWrench and Miss Yasuda, there's anything other you'd like to introduce on this matter?" Both appeared lost as the rest of us. Their responses appeared to have a variety of meanings but settled on "No, Your Honor." Then court is adjourned! The judge orders.

After several days of awaking and having living with my debts, the taste was bitterness. I couldn't sleep, tossing on a slab of rock concrete with a little piece of thin-ass mattress. It's a blessing I hadn't croaked from pneumonia. My feet and toes ol' boy were frozen, splittin' from the cold weather. One quilt that wouldn't reach beyond the knees, windows were busted out from the bitter buckings of the other young gladiators they served those regretful meals three times daily. It was a struggle often to maintain my sanity, partly dealing with layers stripped of my precious freedom and presumptions of innocence. But I vowed not to let my past become decomposed by the days ahead as uncertainty lingered within. Despite this, I followed the rules of Code of Conduct in honor to the letter. "Charm never dissolves." I avoided the old twist monkey wrench, exchanges over those grounded upon principles, upholding my ties at Google brights. Never losing focus, even while of hustling.

Fighting for the ways of dignity and self-decency, it's become uh' new journey, ways of life. Although my perseverance, floated through the air, not to be forgotten, leaving my landmark struck with my handmade carved metal tool. Smoothen out my signature in ghetto graffiti boldly. E.S.O. "East Side Oakland" ya' Ponta Max was in the buildin'. I disavowed to be a could be, yet focused on being the forever, and are, because of what would be's, ah' maybe, and the slight chances of reaching beyond. Thus, for a might have, never was, but uh' has been, was, and are." Signed yours truly "Maxwell Pixar" Afterhourz!"

Time was flying like speedy trials and high-speed chases. Getting transferred wriggling in and outta traffic, awakened by the humid heat of pleasant weather in mid-summer, almost reached into boiling degrees as the blue goose transportation vessels trampled the Dublin Strip. We approached intake's Unit R&R "Receiving and Release." What a sign of relief. "Welcome, guys." The Receiving Officer announced his held presence. A total silence amongst us until voices erupted by some of the wanta-be's, looking to earn a strip or two.

"Right here! I represent the Bay Area. The deep trenches."

"What's your street name?" The officer addressed one of the other inmates.

"Volume. But that's not important, Mr. Officer. I flexed but didn't say anything of poly. Noticing the tension. Step on up, hands behind your back, don't move, or you'll be yesterday's yard conversations." Are you a part of the Bay Area's car? At those instances, he was exercising his authority, taking a different course of action. But I wasn't pressed, nor about to get much involved with any type of nonsense, I peered unmoved. I leaned against the holding tanks' iron gates capturing a glimpse from the other sight boys in the blue.

"Quit asking these ol' police ass questions. Playboy "Volume" heat exchanged between the Officer drilling him.

"What you wanta know next, when's da last time that I Maybach something ? Put his smart ass in the hole!" the jail's captain ordered. "I could give two fucks about going to the hole, you do you. My time's gonna count, whether you eat shit or die." Volume blurted out. "You cocksucker, go sit on your thumb. Let me know what it's tasking like." "Butterfingers?" The officer shoot! Roasting the homey Volume dry, and had the whole room pouring in tears. We laughed until the next shift changed.

"And you'll have those on your meal tray for breakfast first thing in da' morning and dinner too if it's on my watch." Another officer out the squad enjoined in parse, for his panel of partisans interest, yelled aloud, leaving us further slumped, bent outta control in tears of laughter the rest of the evening.

Chapter 19

THE BRIGHT SIDE OF A CANDLE LIT

Departing one housing unit and off to the next was a needed opportunity to get a fresh breather to do some knee-deep soul searching, looking within and reevaluating the actions and behaviors of minds. Thinking life's not supposed to work like this. As I endorsed the reasonings within upon "There gotta' be a better solution to this equation for the roadblocks of a single lifetime." After fourteen tired months confined, I couldn't have been near more than ready for program and or marching down the block yard mainline, which should have happened way before. Though being on my own endorphins. The do you kinda mentality! Simply limiting the "B.S." But still, it hadn't diluted my desires to hit the yard. Representing and programming. Although, as a chess player, moves had to be spanking clean as the board of health with no hitting below the belts, treating yourself worthy a bite of the few bikini lines who'd skate the open lanes. Nurses, free staff were a young boys' dreams.

Other patrons danced through, but there was no room for errors, only progression on the agenda, making calculated steps. Fed up just being uh' pawn in the game. Noticing this, I prioritized for advancing to the next level without being penalized for exercising that hoods mentality. It had its ups and downs. But I pushed forward with a broader cause. Back on the blocks, dorm living was full of adrenaline. Kansas unit, which was considered one of the violent housing dorms. Why? Let me explain. For instance, We were youngest of the yards compound, of course, eighteen and over, different ages from every borough of life. You name it, they housed our kind. Everybody thought they needed to earn a strip, unlike the other units that were designated for the O.Gs. Born in the 70's or above, dudes minding their own bittiness. Unlike the youths, conflating anything we wasn't minding! It was always, blast, if any intuits existed or even a thought, vowed to violate the zones of our comfort. A simple look of any batted eyes could spark riots. Most of the time, our Bay Area's car often was woozy because of ignorance of political strings. Few having the ability to wiggle between different sectors, diffusing situations or applying pressure as needed. The riders understood and spoke particular languages. Nowadays, the youth have resorted to swords and gunplay for any inferences of a disagreed voiced opinion. "Max," known loved by plenty, hated by few, but respected by drowds. Real hitters utilize their differences to establish open lines. Doesn't matter the state, plate, set nor the likes of. There's bridges in everybody's vehicles. Not saying that a compromise at times isn't worth risking. Anyhow, who strives to be set trippin' I acknowledge only two languages, a-go-getter and ah' risk the world and some tryna' ta' get it. You fit into those brackets, you were aliht by your "Ponta Maxwell Pixar." But don't get shit twisted, right or wrong, Momma didn't raise no zombies. If any my homies were outta character, right or wrong. I'm down! Yet, in the same breath, I'll breathe on you. For the wise to prosper often requires checks and of balances. Despite, which foot the shoes on, gotta respect dat!

Almost rise and shine time, as I rebooted while noticing I ain't spoke with Grannie going on two weeks. Knowing she's worried. I'hops on the horn. "Collect. It's your grandson." The recording from AT&T relayed! "My pleasure." Thank you. "Hey momma, how's the famban out there?" "Everybody's doing good and praying for you to get out, but the key is not getting yourself in those kinda situations. I ain't tryin' to be preaching. I prefer you not to find out the hard way. Gotta go. Here's your uncle, who wanna' speak with you. I'm watching my races, ol' Russell Baze, is been some tough today, honey, kicking some butt. Um, um, um! He knows he can ride those dang on horses. He's already done won four races in uh' row today. "What? Did you bet?" Naw, I ain't had no money, child, and too sacred betting. Baby, you know I have utility bills and our rent's due. Here's yo' Uncle." She handed Uncle Fly the horn. Envious, her pockets interceded her from betting.

I knew I needed getting my shit in order to help G'moms out.

"Talk to him. Love you!" "Love you more, Grannie."

"What's up, nephew?" Unk hops on online.

"Ain't too much, Unk. Just being the best I'm able to be. Whether it's heel, sleet, or snow, getting it focused on growth. Keeping it "P.I." (Particular Interesting). You know me, just interviewing work daily."

"Like that! They ain't socking-it-to-your-pockets, Unk."

"Best believe, you know I ain't talking about it, I'm being about it." Unk was forever quick with moves on glues. Prompting my attention to what was on the radars. Hold tight, this my nephew I been getting at you about for the flicks. Perfect opportunity. Danish, this "Max" give him uh' wif on how Fly been wetting these blades round here. Yeah, from San Francisco to Tokyo." The sweetest voice hops online. Why she do that? Um! Jawsn, knowing I'm about to be outta bounds, cause good-n-well I'm not undermining to being one of the first to get with uh' billionaires interior intuitions. Not that money was my sole proprietary idea, but I kinda have a particular whiskey, which I'm admiring–scowling right now through the unit's window panes. Yup, yup!

And she's deserving every bit of Max Pixar, damn right, say that. Yup! I wished only she could see herself the ways I do. "The bright side of a candle lit," having a dude's heart skipping more beats than I'm able to keep up with. Although I'm on the horn engaged with Danish, she's got me nearly half naked watching at a distance. Her actions-readings are shockingly immeasurably da' cutest, even afar, they're likely feeding into her space, which I'm almost certain her womanly scanner picking up my dial, although she's posted bout fifty yards away. It's how well she leaned, cocking her hips, and batted those lids, my gosh! Then darting that stare; like-boy, "What's on my screen looks outta your range hon'." Um! "It looks that way." I fought not to draw, but it wasn't as if it hadn't languished my thoughts. Snap out of it Max, had to not lose the fact Danish was on the other line. Gotta stay focused now, Max, I cautioned myself.

Snap out of it, "pimp suit" had to not lose that Danish was on deck.

"What's your hon?" She bubbly poured out there.

"Sounding like dat, I'ought know why not. What, shouldn't it be? "Purely not Max, forfeiting, I couldn't help but sense uh' brawl.

She dived out there. Was Unk giving Neff uh' test or uh' teaser? I conveyed to myself. This the kinda' jiffy never comes in the boxes. Naw, I didn't bite. Yet, instead went a more Off That Dribble's approach- the substitute hood bounce.

"Danish?"

"Yeah! But your Uncle Fly considers me as nothing other than the truth."

"As he oughta, 'I held saying.' "I heard that! It's uh' good look, damn, sounds like you make a golden combination. Just saying though, some things honestly goes together, tasty as rice and shrimp."

"Um! As if you hadn't noticed." She acted as if I misbehaved. I held my comments dire to myself and wasn't about to be caught whaling. I kinda' answered hers question with a question paraphrasing, looking for the bait, but I didn't get fresh. Instead, I peddled in opposite directions. "Given Unk some recreations out there? That's what's up." Leaving Danish the stage; and she batted a thousand." Lil' Mama opted.

"You know how ya' "Uncle Fly" bee's. Yup got me breaking speed limits getting citations. You know the rituals. "What you implyin'?" I interrupted her mid-sentence, focused to say the least where our conversation was about to lead. I pumped the skates only to save the day. As I admonished, I'm just uh' player baby, and I'm born lace with game" but with you! I'm putting my stunner shades down." "There you is, hmm! Not today. Don't you play wit me, Danish," she teased, just as boo-gee.

"Shit happens, I apologize, but your blessings, that's what I'm built for." Was my only forbidden ultimatum. To be introduced to one of her best friends, something of her pyramid in order to keep hustling off my toes. As ensured. "Danish youz' ah' turbo noch. Who wouldn't be over-inspired had they ignored your kinda speed limits? Just Off The Dribble your intro, I'm leaning. Careful, I ain't tryna' stop you. I'm just being optimistic. Wishful, you might have a twin friend that shares those similar values like yourself." You know I'm unspoken for- but I do have conversation for one, that's if she'll listen, she need not take forever with making her mind up." Have her get with me, Unk, has the hook up."

"Gotcha, I hear ya. They would wanta' move quick with gusto 'cause as you know, it's a drought on winners out here, and this I'm certain, as game it's contagious. "You ain't heard this for free." She didn't respond, but I overstood her silence and idle." Yep, yep! Quite simply then slide her the drift. "Uh' finders on the table."

"Let me quit playing, I know you eighty babies like to stack plenty."

I felt her eyes darting, searching for her next rebound, before she fully finished her final sentence, rerocked my vision. "Say dat then!" She knew instantly, gotta' talking my kinda' shit now.

"Fly, come and get yo' nephew. He's doing way too much!" Oka' we clowning now, Danish?" I could sense her hesitance as if there was more to her wonder, but we didn't visit there. Nothing to dwell on. My only for real intentions were to meeting one of her best friends. We kinda evaded anything other than otherwise. As I hoped to have played, maaabe` well enough leaving a good first impression; it was just the idea and tha' intensity. She woke up my scent game, which wasn't farfetched Oasis, but she was very inspiring, she proffered our par with a taste of "you'll get yours, and that's uh' promise." She nearly drove uh' young dude balistic.

"I just wanna' let you know to enjoy yourself while you're preparing for the days ahead, and I'm waiting and zealous to put a face to our enlightening conversation, keep sharpening those edges, and trust and believe somebody compatible gonna' choose you and take you to victory. Here's your Uncle Fly. You have bright roads in your pathways; don't get distracted." I bounced outta my own way and hit her with my signature hood stare as I caught myself debating.

"There you, wit da' bittiness!" I'm leaving that alone off the table." Unk grabbed the horn as I ensured him no micro- managing was needed. She was only following suit, making sure uh' younging held on solid grounds whereas upon taking deep and drastic measures, in "likewise" strides, while yet holding unto my gangsta. I graph' that Unk was doing the same cheesing, proud of his nephew's initial intro. As I knelt with a taste of humor out of nowhere.

"Yeah, I noticed ol' Danish musta' heard my stomach growling from a thousand yards uh' way." Yet, I envisioned.

"Naw, she's too more consumed with Unk's cohesive upon I contained myself, leaving her bestest upon getting rebounds." A best friend.

"Well, you know I wasn't much surprised. Nothing is; when you moving for real." I kept my thoughts non-political.

"Say Unk, these officers are signaling phone check dial a number for Neph on the other line, kinda' urgent. The area code."

"Hold tight." Nephew.

"Aliht, it's 615." But before I could get the other half of the digits out, Unk interrupts me.

"You know I don't be doing this. I'm gonna' give the horn to your Ponta Maverick."

"Let him handle that."

"Aliiht," Click. Fuck! They hung up the damn phone.

Outta'time!

Chapter 20

MY INTUITIONS

It's the weekend, which means it's a typical family and friends visitation day. Which is a statewide county's mandate. And boy, I'm excited. Haven't seen the fambam, nor my lil ride or die. "Omega Starr," we spoke yesterday in I'ought know how many months, but she's hyped on dippin' through. I have broader and much juicer moves on the agenda. Looking to garnish getting a snap of that ol' glass ceiling. But she ain't knowing. Who cares if it's non-privileged? Meaning, there's not any reasonable expectations of privacy. But it's non-conclusive whether or not they'll have the recorders in motion. I have an intuition but it's uncertain, and I'm about to find out some way or another, whether it's in indirectly or not.

The rooms are positioned right next to each other. The only differences notable, they reserve one of the rooms for legal visitations, attorneys private investigators, and other legal causes, unlike the other rooms, which administer both privileged and non-privacy partakings. Meaning they're open for intruders. But still, who even knows whether the bubbles are live. And that's the unknown around the blocks. It's quietly referred to as the O'Brien's question. Maybe we'll never know. They're not into revealing their hand. That's how they eating, under the radarz, how they utilize it once they've gathered it. That's another question on a different grand subject for a whole other set of equations.

Okay, I'll have to muster, there's not such a thing as reasonable expectations of privacy while engaging with non-legal visits, family, and friends inside a jail's establishment. But the rules differ while you're conversating with any party whose presence are objectionable for the presentations of what's described as none of anybody's business other than attorneys investigator medical practitioners doctors, i.e. As those forms of communications are protected under the status "Privileged Information." And they do not lose safeguard values because one's in custody. You must be protected under pretenses of privileged facets. There's laws that forbids any eavesdropping, and penalties for abrogating those guidelines. It's not difficult.

However, some college PhD scholars would enjoy arguing differently. Given such options, those are the very things that keep me abreast. As I glean-smiling, dancing with a sense of level play, someday might find its home plate. But I'll pursue forward, thankful for another day; that's what's inviting about experiences. We live to learn while pursuing on. I wear no strains from behind. Nor do I consider my yesterdays as turbulences that hadn't manifested. Instead, I'm welcoming opportunities for a lifetime's journey. I'm visualizing value with a unifying approach, in hindsight, an idea of what's become my self's mirror purest form. I've had to ask if a subject looks undisrupted, yet everything around elsewhere appears brightly in within features, opposite the reflections, "Now what does that ring?" A landscape of opportunities? Who wouldn't realize the displayed visuals, "How sweet, what's being spoken for.?"

Okay, so what if they've got an third eye popping ? Who gives uh', they'll likely soon go distances. That's only if fortunate enough! Let's aim our questions geared "TMZ". Hope the nod filters viral. Lucky for us right? Might could utilize uh' promo after this bid. Few extras ain't never hurt anybody I knew. "Ready, bright lights, action!" Naw, we ain't rocking that, I'm just saying though. I mean, I mean! Can a young player live one time? Although they say the world's disengaged, yet it's our society punishing folks for what not they believe is unfair, depending on who you are, they're revoking ghetto cards for dudes fighting back, I heard the hell outta' that! Wthout doubt, they got action every time with me cause dat's what's up! Detect the scent, It's what we do good. I'm counting money with my bright lights glowing, I'ought know about you, but I'm uninterested keeping score on the renegade zones?

They got it designed "in my opinion, and set up for golden foreplay. The units visiting booths off to the side, one on ones, except for the blinds open if some asshole wanta' be bold or nosey, o'well push on. It's jail gotta' take the good with da' unfortunates. Only thing, there's a divider between us. But uh' little bit of glass ain't never prevented me from doing nothing I didn't wanta' do. And damn sho' not getting no lochie. How mindful; tasteful they co-polite Mr. "Bubble Butt." I cautioned myself while preparing for the extravagances. Freak show visit with "Ms. Omega Starr." I'm not trippin', I'mm' do me flying under the tinted radarz. Although I'm unable to dissect the dial, whether or not there's a video cannon's on deck behind "ol' bubble butt" the rooms' device for monitoring. It's configured like the size of an pencil lead. Tucked underneath tents tripple black, the bubbles rounded off underneath disguise, you'd not look twice at. It's only noticeable if you're inspecting. You know the saying. "Don't go looking for trouble. You'll find it." But this feels in opposite and yells the very symptoms of justice! Still the restraints aren't visible. That's unjust to surreptitiously record a person's making promos without approvals. And then acting as if there's absent measurable taints… holding straight brights deserves an Oscar. That's the only reason I'm paying homage towards the Red Carpet. Letting the world know dignity tired of being overworked and underpaid. Keep ya' mind leveled while you sippin' "X.O." out the arch of the prints, ahold still. Damn right, let's neutral those dimensions." Who gives uh' damn, mightiest well. Yep, say that!

I'ought want no smoke," but down to shadowbox with bright whites, and if they run up on me, yeah, I'm prepared for street fighting. If it gets too dirty, I'm discharging my Constitutional Rights. This not uh' video shoot make believe, we're speaking real physical images and of a person's civil liberties. Who signed for dat? I hadn't! Nor the least bit do I acknowledge any offered waivers. My attorney althoughs Pro Bono, a hippy type, you know the kind, got the swagger of uh' Tony Serra attorney at law, down going distances for his clients even uh' take a jail sentence himself. We fought tooth and nail up against the best of, blow for blows, ringing the horns. Didn't help. The Judge was vigorously wondering in his own world. Like are you serious? I'm just putting it out there, asking the unanswered. What's da' standards for "quid pro"? Better yet, who's paying attention of those who cheated us how they dividing *those* potlucks. As it's known, money comes in different formats, as Bitcoins proved beyond speculations. I'm not tryna' be overly political. But, I overstood my nonwaiver Miranda Rights. There's not an excuse that'll justify reasons for having any conversations with any counsel placed under video cameras absent our knowledge. "Who does that?" Like, for real, quit playing!

You wanta' present the defense for a trial of my life, you're expecting that we should openly disclose our plans in front of our opponents, and then thinking I'm never supposed to question identity." I'm like, who are you? And you said.."Huh! huh! huh! I didn't; wait a minute, sir. I didn't understand your question the first time." Do you know my attorney had an audacity to try and visit me one day, and he was dressed in his Hawaii shirt and short pants matching with a straw hat, looking so Miami Vice. Appearing getting ready to engage in a drug bust. Good thing soonest I pried into the booths visiting room, peeped out the scenery I waived. "Good- bye." Didn't even bother going that direction. From then on he knew my quest forward. It read through his facial features, insinuating. "You know it looks like cover's blown guys." Now, at this level of the game, do I invoke the right of self- representation? There's no way in the world we're about to engage with any further dialogue. Better yet, nor any other counsel, investigator or the likes of not under those kinda restraints. That was out! Might as well phone up San Quentin guilty upon as charged on arrival. Good thing counsel overstood his duties.

Back in the courtroom for a Motion For Recusal, instead, they substituted a stand-in counsel, a second attorney, Merlyn Price, to help Mr. GoodWrench resolve our hideous language barriers. What a thoughtful, pricey mission for neutralizing our hurdles. But that was only a portion of our plentiful disputes. I found they intended to distract from the root of our infusions. My mind was completely made up. There wasn't anything she could have said that would have detoured what I believed whether we were under watch *without* a valid search warrant. If she'd objected or misguided the facts and, or undermined those assumptions. Our relationship was over right there! As I fired one counsel due to the same confrontations and hadn't required much for her to be next. I motioned to Ms. Merlyn Price during our visitation, "Imma' be right back," got up just as politely surveyed the rooms' perimeters, which was only an 8'10" structure. Again, there sat that little black bubble dancing. You know I didn't stir up no drama, though wasn't worth causing any type of commotion. Plus, maintaining respect works best both ways. As it appeared she was capable of detecting our mental barriers through a similar lens, to assert and or initiate our nonwaivers under surveillance was unwarranted. My perspective again, humans we're recorders and can reboot whatever we visualize upon command upon any given stages. Now, I'm like, OK. Maybe there's a reason for her obnoxiousness. "Reluctantly," I asked her if she'd notify the units deputies that our conference upon commenced. She did as asked. Shown partly *braveness* of character, highly appreciated, non- confrontational licensed to be. Right off hand, I found encouraging, and inhaled a breath of fresh air. I flushed. Hum!

Maybe she isn't as your practical public defender, irrespective she was pro bono's hired help. And a hippie, which was viewed informal for givin' me uh' sense of relief. We often adjust like hammers on knocks, ready for that rapidness until our jobs finished gleaming and itching for the boards, like who wants da' bitterness! Recognizing we were speaking an identical effective language, non-verbal communication, which is fluent in the hood as ghetto Ebonics for preferences, upon conversating.

Our legal meetings were becoming somewhat alarming for defending my positions. Why routinely the same hours weekly? I held my panic button, listened to her agenda. I focused. But wasn't sold on P.D's. "Public Pretenders." I gotta note: Whom I never quit understood, I kinda' managed the gauge against P.Ds risk of consequences, playing my mitts close-ranged. But she hadn't struck the type who was on a different frequency, but it's known looks can be deceiving. That's the reason court offers exhibits, upon altering perceptions. I gathered no differences from the visuals of her appearance. Holding those thoughts in place, drawing my own inferences. Keep in mind, Mr.

Bubble Butts' lens was placed like directly strained on her back and to my fronts. Ms. Merlyn Price, hadn't appeared the least intimidated by the surroundings, I kinda gotten offended. Because services of hers were under my desires, meaning she consisted of hired help, and not the other way around. And could be replaced. But notwithstanding, her actions held my interest of wishes. Kindly was a hell of a byproduct. I considered her indispensable, Kosher. Her vehicle services favored as a luxury rental car being driven properly by its valid license driver, being that myself. Noticing how court orders required to search and seize one's personal property. I oppose. Attorneys are seen as vehicles- machines. Preventing any harm while foreseeably assisting the goals they're hired for, enunciating their effective assistance of counsel. In the actual process, if disrupted in achieving those objectives, that's ah' no way space brainer, due process violation. In fact, it's a search and seizure of property. As long as those physical barriers prevent our openly two-way communication, doesn't Jeopardy attach? Somebody then deserves an outstanding warrant. Isn't justice required to hold its harmony? "Mr. Sheriff, maybe you're driving on the wrong side of the roads doing 60 MPH in a designated zone for 30 MPH. Where's your license? Now the shoe's on opposite, the rules deviate and to whom's benefits? It's unheard of, right?

Explain yourself sir. Uh. Citizen's arrest, you heard those terms before.

Chapter 21

OWNERSHIP RIGHTS

You know it's against the law to pull someone's vehicle over and seize their actual possessions. Attorney's actions are private and may be considered personal property. And then to enforce a criminal proceeding, is not that two forms of punishment? You can only do one or the other. Either relinquish my personal property and or prosecute. But you're not permitted to have our cake and ice cream too, I do believe. But I might be wrong. My counsel's hand motions, thoughts, opinions, knowledge given plus, received is preserved under attorney client's privileges. For which unlawfully eavesdropping that's uh' Federal crime. And the data on her laptop, thoughts of which couldn't be fully prowled through. Is in my opinion a confiscation of personal property at the very least. In fact, you can keep it. It's no use to us once you've seized and prevented me from capitalizing on its held purposes.

How it supposedly works: once a person's property is under siege, counsel, due to restraints I couldn't maintain ownership rights. Therefore, the vehicle wasn't it detained. Likewise myself. You may not authorize a person, such an attorney, then sabotage those rights under false pretenses in the absence of a valid court's order must not probe. Further, you must give a party "forfeiture notices" enabling the return for his or her's property upon it's contested with verifiable ownership rights. The attorney's preferences are listed whom they are obligated. There's a record kept of dates and times to my knowledge. And yeah, I would indeed appreciate another look- "Fresh out the bar."

Assume you're engaged with an unlawful brush of misdeeds, violation. Your property gets tangled and seized, pieces of real estate, cars, jewelry or the likes of. You're entitled to that absolute right to claim your belongings, if it's yours and you've rightfully acquired such. You may certainly petition your interest within a reasonable time, or it'll become states' property forfeited. It's non-refundable. They'll likely auction the assets. But you'll get the forfeiture notices, and you must decide what's in your best interest. If it's related to trap money, it wouldn't be smart to oppose those seizures. Then you mighta' gotten one of those forms of context with a personal relationship, which predates the cause of actions. I wouldn't be discouraged. Say you're lawfully a couple, and they leverage possession of your spouse, and require you to answer under conspiracy, you might wanta inquire whether or not that's multiple punishments for the same offense. "Double Jeopardy." They'll have to release her or you before prosecution is legal. The actual fear of abuse of such contents are enough, which invokes a seizure. Utilizing those aspects, control over a person's property, absent a search warrant or judge's orders, isn't that punishment in itself. Jeopardy, shouldn't it attach? A person may have possession of something although not holding it in a physical form, which rises to the level of controlled ownership. And qualifies, in my belief a seizure of a person's property. It's irrelevant what a person has done. You may not punish a person twice and keep on for the exact same overt acts. This includes if you've done a violation of hit and run, hurt a pedestrian, and you were driving in a stolen vehicle." Regardless, gestures of forfeiture are contestable, not the vehicle. But let's assume your personal property is in the trunk of that vehicle; you may have the right to have your possessions returned based on "double jeopardy." And or the latter. This is a question for whom?

Another notion: say you're being detained and held to answer, your place of residence was raided, they seized your funds at your stash house. Stacks, jewelry, and other tangibles you've worked for. You have receipts of purchase. But it's taken and listed under evidence. Although, during related times, they're threating the forfeiture of your personal property and valuables and forcing you to answer upon charges, holding the assets above your head. That's "multiple punishments. Isn't it not?" As they should either play or fish the bait. But not having their unlimited swipes, that's not the score. I'm only saying that to say if you're being punished, placed under physical restraints, and prevented from defending against an opposition, wouldn't you diagnose that as multiple punishments? But they not playin' fair, and too on renegade time, kinda. But you ought gotta' pay me no mind.

To be continued

HOUSE REPS publishing presents
BEYOND
Worth uh' Dance
THE GOVENOR

Chapter 1

SOME TIMES THE BEST IS UNSAID

They say it's cheaper biting a bullet sometimes than spitting one, and I'm not about to argue about the differences of opinions; it's facts, not fiction. Yet these folks out here on this other side of the bridge don't in hindsight have any practical realities about life. It's amazing those shackles they indirectly utilize. But okay. It's the wealthiest county surrounding our Bay Area. I wondered why, but now I'm learning. They hustling under the radar. Welcome to the Land of the A's they doing lap dances, tossin' Rock Stars by stares while sipping X.O Outta the arch of mittens standing still! Unlike the typical who of deviates, before lunch hour, I dial "Omega Star" my ride or die; Good work. She's always ready for the deepest levels the game prescribes, and today it's sho' nuff visiting she pose ta' slide through. Boy, I'm praying she's not dry cappin, and solo-bolo, riding alone. Yeah, I'mm Uh' find out what it don't. "Ms. Bubble Butt," I whispered under my breath. "They about to get their opportunities to have an eyeful, I'm almost certain it's game-thieving going on in those visiting booths." This is about to determine the fragrance they rocking behind tents. If I'm lucky, just might have something for Ms. Jessica Jackson and Dream Corps. Fresh offa the barz uh' Class Action Suit. Let those eyes answer the horn underneath the tented windows of Ms. Bubble Butt. I'll know soonest.

"Mr. Maxwell Pixar, you have a visitor in room B. Your half- hour starts once you enter the open doors." The floor deputy announces over the unit's intercom. I'm nervous as hell, thinking to myself, "Please let that be ol' Omega Star," I mumbled to myself out loud while putting the finishing dabs on my well-kept silky waves, dipping so hard you coulda' pushed a wave runner jet ski on those oceans. Just finished with my thousand push-ups an hour ago plus lotioned up those bedroom abs, looking like uh' runway model ready for ah' Drew House or Reebok commercial. Her little jukebox gone be knocking da' most I hinted. Okay, Max, it's about dat time fa' rise and shine, grabbing my plastic from today's lunch, squirted a pinch of Jergens body lotion right in that thang. Stay ready you ain't gotta get ready. It's about to get jiggy; lil momma Ms. Omega and I ain't laid eyes on each other going on six months. She's been bluffin of practicing celibacy since going on New Year's, I'm like Aliiht! But good. Lucky for us, yeah right! But I'mm give her the benefit of the doubts why knock her for having herself ah' New Year's resolution. Life's precious, if she's keeping that vault shut, there's rewards for exercising pause buttons. That's uh' good thang, I'm dancing in circles finding myself pacing for oxygen, preparing for this visit. My body's processing my desires of what if Omega read my intentions over the telephone during our last conversation yesterday, and she comes fully equipped to serenade like uh' hungry piranha, anxious to run that, we rockin.' Okay, showtime. As I enter those visiting rooms gates, I'm greeted by lil momma; looking so aggressively sexy. I gleamed over her voluptuous figure while searching for a proper ice breaker to set the vibes on non-orthodox relaxations, in intimate zones. Within seconds I found her body language peering through the glass and onto my lap. Woooh! And she was flyin so- lo-bo-low. I almost lost my mind, but I caught myself. Calm it down, Maxwell. Hold tight now. Do not spill the whisky. Sparks flew, but I didn't lose contentious as I hadn't wanted appearing overly excited, but Damn! Everything was in the right places, and I mean everything from her French toes to her "*whatchamacallit eyes.*" Which as I moved to be seated without looking away from her tender thighs; which spoke of a complete different language than her tone of voice. Explicit with a drift of force of nature, as I perceived something more promising about her every time her hips adjusted positions. The only thing that I could say was, "*Damn,* you about to make this very hard on both us!" After she'd thoroughly undressed me without even speaking a single awe, somehow, I still managed to lever what was obvious to become subtle, yet futile. Hell, I completely forgot about Ms. Bubble Butt dancing to its own rhythm behind the tents, as my unopposed attention had me rethinking the dial of her ring finger, leaving my thoughts frozen, flirting with outlandish possibilities. Not excluding the reasons for her upon deciding to wear a button-down pullover, four sizes too big, perfect timing and place. As I declared my gauge, slightly harassing, leaving the options for her to splash without causing huge waves, registering to the sound bites of the alarms that not only mines, but most men with any kinda taste buds vigorously answers to.

"You always outshine the globe sunshine, don't you?" I boldly reclaimed, interrupting our silence. Omega Star almost sorta paraphrased in thoughts; of what it seemed she was about to say, upon me drawing a smile outta her, instead, her reactions were a hidden fetish that I overwhelmingly considered to be somehow mines. *BINGO!* She unleashes, opening her wardo's garment, and the treasuries outta nowhere stared out at attention saving the day, aimed centered into my dilated pupils. I knew we were on a time limit, it was just my recreational reflexes. "Thirty minutes only gon' torture you," Omega whispers, barely growling, nearly almost inaudible to be heard aloud to avoid any disturbance from alerting the unit's other inmates, while not aware of any aspects of her co- pilot flying above us. Ms. Bubble Butt. She quickly closed her blinds before giving any opportunities to fantasize with a blip.

"Do as you please, lil mama," I *blushed* upon her actions, revealing the Jergens outta my lunch wrappings, as I positioned it on the table Just letting her know I came ready to party. Please don't stop da' music Let's dance! Despite the fact that we could be likely under surveillance from the hidden eyes of Ms. Bubble Butt, we still hadn't done nothing to dodge off any routine ops from peering. I wasn't about to interrupt our vibe, though. They'd just gotta do some paperwork; I'm already in the hole drenched, they can't woop my ass! At best, I might just lose a lil pod time. And! But I wasn't about to floss too hard though, bringing out the hammer, ya da' mean. In my opinion, why jeopardize this lap dance lil moma going hamm! And doing the fool, closing her eyes trying to find something. I'ought know what she'd misplaced. But boy, she was active like uh' knock with a strobe light. "Do what you do, lil mama."

I posed, inviting our good time. "Okay, I'm almost there." Omega Star pleaded just as quietly. You wouldn't have thought in a million light years we weren't someplace other than a Hilton 5-Star Palace, given how peacefully she was seated opposite the windowpanes. "Is it almost noon yet?" I quizzed, but she didn't answer.

"Have you found whatever you're looking for?" Again, she was wide-eyed, but not unattached. "This kinda' stare, I'll fess up, it's not for just everyone to gleam, or it could spread like uh' bad dream." She paraded on as if she wasn't able to speak, with an agenda very likely about to go viral, that's if my insinuations of the unknown were correct. Ms. Bubble Butt was dancing in its own corner.

Out of nowhere, Omega responded with da' sexiest facial features and silent cries, which spoke of a different measure. Letting out huffs and puffs, catching her breath before speaking.

"Woooh! Why did you need something?" Mustering that violet look in her eyes that matched my next unspoken thoughts. "I wanna' lap dance, wasn't busy or too busy tossin' Rock Stars by glares."

"Poppi you proud of me?" She fought not to ask. I obnoxiously insisted on her to give da' time, but she respectfully declined to answer. Like she always does, brandishing that faithful coined signature proceeding forward with lines of her own questions while unstudied of the time.

"You thought I wouldn't answer the horn if you dialed?" I inquired further while she of defended her positions—I filtered.

"You never disappoint anytime you know margins on the line, that's what I admire about you Omega." Quickly I urged her to explain herself. Which, although I like to believe that I'm a multitasker, was busy focusing on the greater substance, the dinner not the dessert. Luckily, I hadn't lost my thoughts while placing my heels into the visiting booth, during the same breaths clutching ahold of my ghetto card- of which I'd been eagerly waiting for the right time to draw. Letting the four levels characters fully soak, reclining with my hustler sponge out, active and attentive. Didn't even have to apply the Jergens and score that touchdown. If that's not winning! Before getting out what was on my tongue, the deputy inside our living quarter's floor panel yelled, "Mr. Pixar, your time's up sir!" Now mind you I'm locked under the radars for possession of a concealed weapon charges, and like always, they got me wrapped up on parole since way when. As the bailiff yells, time's up, Mr. Pixar, I'm like damn, time surely flies when you're handling some business. I answered.

"Aliiht, about to wrap it up." I motioned into the living unit quarter's corridors giving lil' mama the final opportunity to finish collecting her bright thoughts.

"You know it's in your court now, make your next move our best news!" Omega ferociously insisted while she dipped from her seat, getting ready to spin off. I assured her, "I'mma keep 20/20 visions over those thongs. I like bout, bout it chic's know how to answer- they score!" Brandishing that twinkling sensitive heart stare which signified, "only in due time!" But she wasn't lost for words. Insisting, "You know to love Omega, means only you're sure of yourself." Those heels were born idle for Lamborghinis, pulling up into Fleetwood cribs fully decored, tucked somewhere off da' coast in a lavish spread. Unleashing her golden wink, implying, you just watch, I'mm bring you da' bitness! Was of the way she ended our visitation. Then leaving my response surveying her imagination at the deepest of its realms, leaning on the edge of my angelicas, yet seizing her up and down as a body language expert "Blanca Cobbs" woulda. Before concluding um! Feeling some other kind of way. Although speechless, I didn't know whether I needed to respond to those of pleasing rhetorics. My internal instincts commanded, but sometimes the best is unsaid. I vowed on rebounds looking the other way into the days ahead, noticing provisional roads to the Oscars don't always require you to reveal the routes veered. There's known ecstasy often finding a balance with a gentle hold. I'ought know about you, but I'm delighted by life's daily struggles and those who are rooting for you, whether you won or lost. If they bottled that up into a single fragrance titled "Notice" presented by Golden for Men and Maxwell for women, you think that'll fly off the shelves?

www.ingramcontent.com/pod-product-compliance
Lightning Source LLC
Chambersburg PA
CBHW051506170626
46811CB00002B/683